FRIGHT TIME

3 Spine-tingling Tales
for Young Readers

- THE WHITE PHANTOM
- NIGHTMARE NEIGHBORS
- CAMP FEAR

BARONET
B·O·O·K·S

Baronet Books, New York, New York

FRIGHT TIME

edited by
Rochelle Larkin and Joshua Hanft

THE WHITE PHANTOM

by Eve Marko

1

The footprints were big. *Real* big.

I noticed them right away because it rained last night. They were animal prints in the hard mud, the biggest I've ever seen.

I was on my way to Hunter Ridge, but now I stopped and looked all around me. Nothing made a sound. Below I could see the blue water of Hurley Creek. Up above, Hunter Ridge was full of trees and forests.

I looked down at the ground again. Who—or what—made these tracks?

All around me, the bushes were flattened out.

Some were even cut in half, as if some gigantic animal had come rushing through the forest and trampled them down. The tracks came down from up on the ridge and then back up again. I looked down a second time and saw the gray stones of our house just below the hill.

This is crazy, I thought. If I didn't know better I could swear some gigantic animal had stood here last night and looked down at our house!

I looked at those footprints again. They were much bigger than my feet. They were much bigger than my *dad's* feet. I knew there were deer in these forests, but it wasn't some deer that had made these tracks. It was something else. Something I'd never seen before.

There was a noise behind me. I jumped. A family of wild turkeys came into the clearing where I was standing. They stopped when they saw me, but since I just stood there watching them, they continued on their way down to the creek, probably to have a drink of water.

I'd never seen wild turkeys this close before. They were big purple and gray birds with long red necks and angry red eyes. I looked down at their feet as they passed. Their feet were tiny compared to whatever it was that made the enormous tracks in the hard mud.

Something hit the ground in front of me with a loud crunch. It was a small rock and it landed just three feet from where I stood.

Suddenly there was a loud commotion. The wild turkeys squawked loudly and flapped their wings hard as they rose up to the trees, disappearing as fast as they could.

"Did I get any?" a voice asked from behind the trees.

A girl came running into the clearing and looked up at the birds that were flying away. She wore shorts and a T-shirt, a red and white L. A. Dodgers baseball cap, and red sunglasses. "Did I hit any?"

"You almost hit *me*," I said. "Are you crazy, throwing a rock like that? You could have hurt somebody!"

She looked at me through her red sunglasses. "Why would anybody just be standing there looking at a bunch of birds?" she asked, shrugging her shoulders.

"I've never seen wild turkeys this close before," I told her. "And I'm not anybody, I'm Andy Baker. I just moved here yesterday."

"Are you the family that moved into that big

stone house at the bottom of the hill?"

"That's us."

I put out my hand. She put out hers.

"I'm Jenny Humphreys," she said, "but everybody calls me Shades on account of my sunglasses."

We shook hands. I looked down at her arm.
There was a big Band-Aid around her elbow and
a couple of long scratches up and down her arm.
"Shades, you look like you play football," I told
her.

She smiled. She wore braces on her upper
teeth but you could tell that nobody dared tease
her about them. "I play everything, especially
baseball," Shades said. "But I got these scratches because I spend a lot of time up on the Ridge.
Only sometimes when it's dark I can't see where
I'm going." She had a blade of grass in her mouth
and she started chewing on it.

"You walk up here in the dark?"

"Sure," she said. "What's the matter, are you
afraid of the dark?"

"Don't be such a smart aleck," I told her. Then
I remembered the footprints. "Hey, Shades, what
do you think of this?" I showed her the footprints
in the hard mud.

6

You never saw anybody's face change as fast as hers did when she saw those footprints. The blade of grass fell out of her mouth and her face got all white. Then she took off her sunglasses and bent down to stare closely at the big tracks. When she looked up at me her eyes were big and brown and something else. They were scared.

"What's it doing down here?" she whispered.

I swallowed hard. I wasn't sure I heard right. "What's what doing down here?"

"The Phantom," she said. "The White Phantom." She stepped back from the tracks as if she were afraid.

"The White Phantom?"

She looked down at the footprints again. "It's never been this far down before," she whispered. She clenched her hand hard and I noticed she was shaking.

"Shades," I said. When she still didn't answer, I shook her shoulder. "Shades! What's the White Phantom?"

Finally she looked at me. "It's a white dog," she said in a strange, quiet voice. "A huge white dog, the biggest you ever saw. Only it's not a dog."

Now I was really confused. A huge white dog that's not a dog? "It's got to be one or the other,"

I told her. "It's a dog or it's not a dog."

"It's a spirit," she whispered. "A spirit that takes the shape of an enormous white dog. A monster."

Her hand was really shaking now. I couldn't believe it. "That's crazy," I said.

"I know it sounds crazy but it's not. Everybody around here knows about it. It protects the Indian burial grounds on the hills above the ridge. Years ago the Seneca Indians lived in this valley. They buried their dead in the hills right above us. The White Phantom protects the Indians who are buried there."

I looked at her. Ghosts! Spirits! Monsters! A phantom that protects Indian burial grounds. Was she for real?

She'd stopped shaking, but I could see she was still scared. I looked down at the tracks again. They *were* huge. No animal I knew made tracks that big.

The sun had set. It was suddenly dark in the clearing. The trees waved in the wind and leaves crunched on the ground. It was Labor Day and the leaves were already falling.

Now I was starting to get nervous. "Spirits don't make tracks," I told her.

"This one does. It howls. It walks in those hills. It even kills." She looked at me. "Andy, whatever you do, don't ever go up there."

"Up where?"

She nodded her head in the direction of the hills. "Up to the burial grounds. Up by the big oak and the Cave of the Dead. The White Phantom will kill you. I mean it."

The big oak! The Cave of the Dead! I looked at Shades. The panic in her eyes was starting to get to me. I was starting to feel funny. My hands were cold and my mouth was dry. A real wind was blowing now. More leaves were falling hard on the ground.

Suddenly, a long low howl broke into the quiet.

Shades jumped to my side. I would have jumped, too, but my legs were frozen to the ground.

"What's that?" I asked quickly.

"It's him," she whispered. "The Phantom. It always howls after sunset."

"Where is it?" I asked her, whispering now, too.

"It's on the hills above the ridge. There it goes again," Shades said, frightened as the howling began again. She turned. "I've got to go home."

"No, wait!" I said. Something was bothering me. "You say you've heard it before?"

She nodded.

"Have you ever seen it?"

She paused, then nodded again.

"Where?"

"Up in the hills."

Now I knew what was bothering me. I grabbed her arm. "You said it's always up in the hills," I said to her. "But then what was it doing down here last night? What are these footprints doing here?"

Her eyes grew even bigger and her face got whiter. "I don't know," she whispered. "It always stayed up in the hills before."

"But these footprints show it came down the ridge last night. That's why you're frightened, isn't it?"

She looked me in the eyes. "It never did this before." She looked down at the footprints, then down the hill, then up at me again. "Last night it came down here and stared down at your house. I don't know what it was looking at or who it was looking for. I just know it never came down here before."

We both jumped again. The howling was even louder this time.

"It was looking at that window," Shades said when it stopped, pointing at the only window in our house that you could see from the ridge. "Whose window is that?" she asked.

I broke into a sweat even though it was no longer warm.

"Mine," I said.

2

I caught Shades by the arm just as she was about to run.

"I got to go," she said, "it's getting late."

"Hold on a minute," I told her, but she wasn't listening. She pulled her arm away and was about to go when I saw something shining on the ground. Quickly I picked it up.

"You dropped your sunglasses, Shades," I said.

"Give them to me."

"First tell me what happened when you saw the White Phantom."

She hesitated. "I will if you give them to me."

I gave the glasses to her and she put them on. She looked down at the footprints and then back at me. "Remember I told you that I liked to walk up here at night?"

I nodded.

"Well, a couple of weeks ago I walked down this ridge to the path that leads into the hills. I wasn't going to go to the burial grounds, I'm not *that* crazy. In fact, I was turning around to go home. And then I saw it. It was all the way up the path between the trees."

"What did it look like?"

"I told you. It's shaped like a dog and it's white as snow, but it's huge. It's a monster."

"What did you do?"

She stared at me. "*Do*? Are you crazy? I didn't do anything. I was so petrified I couldn't move. Then it disappeared."

"What do you mean, it disappeared?"

"Just what I said, it disappeared."

I looked at her suspiciously. "Are you sure it was there to begin with?"

She crossed her hands across her chest. "Andy Baker, for your information, I don't see things that aren't there. What about the howling? Are you going to tell me we didn't hear that either?"

She had a point there. We listened. The howling seemed to have stopped, for now.

"Look, Shades," I said. "I'm not saying you're lying. I just don't believe in spirits or ghosts."

"That's because you're not from around here."

"That's true, but I do know something about Indians. Dad even says one of our ancestors was a Mohawk Indian. Here, take a look at this." I opened the collar of my shirt.

"What is it?" she asked, looking at what I held in my hand.

"It's a chain. A chain of wampum beads. And not just any beads either. These are black wampum beads. Only the greatest Mohawk warriors wore black wampum beads. They've been in our family for generations. When I turned 12 last month, Dad gave the chain to me to wear around my neck."

"Can I touch them?" she asked.

I let her hold them in her hand.

"There were Mohawks in this valley many years ago," Shades said. "Maybe your ancestor, that Mohawk warrior, lived here. Maybe he was even buried here after he died in the Cave of the Dead."

"What's the Cave of the Dead?" I asked her.

"It's a big cave above the ridge in the middle of the burial grounds. It goes deep under the hills. When the Indian warriors knew they were going to die, they would go to the cave and wait there. When they died, their family went up to bury them. That's why it's called the Cave of the Dead. Nobody has ever come out of it alive."

"Have you ever gone in there, Shades?"

She let go of the beads and said angrily, "I told you, Andy, nobody goes there. *Nobody*."

"Are you sure?"

She shook her head. "Listen, Andy," she said. "Don't do something stupid. Don't go up to those hills. Stay away from the burial grounds. And whatever you do, don't go to the Cave of the Dead. If you do, *you'll* never come back. The White Phantom will see to that."

We said good-bye and she left.

The walk home took only 15 minutes, but it was almost dark and I was real nervous. There are lots of sounds in the dark that aren't there during the day. Every once in a while I turned and looked over my shoulder, but nothing was there.

When I got home and we had dinner I told Mom and Dad about the burial grounds in the hills, though not about the White Phantom. I didn't know what they'd think if I told them about that. Dad said that about six different Indian tribes lived in this valley many years ago. He said it's bad luck to walk on the burial grounds without respect.

We all went to bed after dinner. I guess everybody was tired because of the move. But I couldn't sleep. I kept on thinking of what Shades had said about the White Phantom. Everybody knows there are no such things as ghosts and spirits, I thought. Maybe what Shades saw that night was just a big dog. There are lots of big dogs around.

But what about the footprints, I wondered. What could have made those footprints?

I thought I'd never fall asleep. But I probably did because some time later—don't ask me how much later—I opened my eyes. I didn't know what had woken me up, but something did. Something quiet and mysterious. Something outside.

I lay in my bed, listening hard. At first all I could hear were regular night noises like the sound of the alarm clock by my bed, the wind in the trees, the honking of the ducks in Hurley Creek, the leaves falling to the ground. But the leaves weren't just falling. Something seemed to be falling on *them*, stepping on them. Footsteps.

Now I was completely awake. Someone— something—was outside. The footsteps were soft and slow but I could hear them crunching up the leaves. Closer and closer they came to the window and now I could hear breathing. It was loud and heavy. No dog I knew breathed like that. Could it be the Phantom?

And then the breathing got softer and I heard the footsteps again. It was moving away from the house, away from me.

I hurried out of bed, and went downstairs and across the living room. I opened the front door as quietly as possible so that Mom and Dad wouldn't hear, and stepped out onto the deck.

Then I heard a scream.

It was loud and terrible. A cry of fear and agony and something else. Horror.

Then it was quiet once again, so quiet that for a moment I wondered if I'd imagined it. I looked up to see if the light had gone on in my parents' bedroom. Nothing. They hadn't heard a thing. I listened again. It was *too* quiet now. The ducks were not honking anymore. They'd heard the scream, too.

But where did it come from?

I walked toward the steps. There, behind the deck, was our underground root cellar. Mom had pointed it out to me yesterday when we first moved and explained that we could store our vegetables there. It was buried under the big rocks that went up the ridge.

That's where the sound had come from.

I went down the steps and toward the cellar. I looked across the grass. There was a half-moon out and many stars, which gave a lot of light. I looked to the sides and up the slope, but there was nothing. Whatever it was must have gone away. It seemed safe.

I reached the root cellar. It was a big hole in the ground. As soon as I peered inside I knew I should have brought a flashlight, because it was completely dark inside. I knelt down on the ground and put my head inside, but I still couldn't see anything. I'm going to have to come back in the morning, I thought, crawling back out and raising my head.

I stopped and sat still. Stiller than I had ever sat in all my life.

The rocks on top of the root cellar were white in the moonlight. But as I looked up, they darkened. All around me the grass grew darker and darker as a black shape rose behind me. I could see my shadow on the ground, but behind my shadow was a much bigger shadow, dark and huge, so huge that it swallowed up my shadow and made everything black.

It was standing right behind me!

I closed my eyes.

I could feel its breath on the back of my neck. My knees shook so hard I thought I'd fall down to the ground. It was a cool night but that didn't matter, the sweat just poured down my back. I put my hand up and touched the black beads around my neck. I waited for something, I didn't know what. Maybe the feel of its hot mouth on my face, maybe the touch of its teeth on my neck.

It waited, too. It stood behind me, waiting. Its hot breath chilled me all over. My fingers, my hands, every part of my body trembled and shook. I wanted to scream. I tried, but nothing came out of my mouth. I was so scared I couldn't scream, I couldn't even make a sound. I could hardly even breathe.

I waited for something—a leap, a terrible roar. But nothing happened. My eyes stayed closed. Any minute now, I thought, any minute.

I don't know how long I crouched like that. I don't know how long I waited. Finally I knew I'd have to do something. With my eyes still closed, I started counting to ten very, very slowly. At the count of ten I was going to turn around. I didn't want to. Turning around and seeing that thing was the last thing I wanted to do. But I couldn't wait any longer. I counted to ten, opened my eyes and turned around real fast.

There was nothing there.

I looked right and left. There was moonlight on the grass again. The rocks on top of the root cellar were white. There was no shadow there, no shadow anywhere.

But it couldn't have been just a shadow, I thought. Or was it?

I looked up at the forest that covered the ridge. Could it have been something simple, like maybe a big tree that shook in the wind, whose shadow fell on the stones and the grass? No way, I thought. There really had been something there. Something really had stood behind me, something big, something dangerous. I could feel it. I just knew it.

But what was it?

I looked at the dark root cellar. I'll find out tomorrow, I thought. Tomorrow when it gets light, I'm going to look inside. Something had happened. There had been a scream. Tomorrow I'd find out what it was.

I went inside and went back to bed. I didn't want to fall asleep, I wanted to wait for the sun to come up so that I could go and take a look inside the root cellar. But I ended up falling fast asleep, because the next time I opened my eyes the sun was up in the sky and everything looked so bright and cheerful you wouldn't have guessed what had happened the night before.

It was the first day of school. Mom made me a big breakfast, with cereal and eggs and lots of toast. I finished it all up. I was so starved. Then I hurried outside.

I felt funny as I walked to the root cellar. I wasn't sure the scream really happened the night before. Could it have been a dream, I asked myself.

It wasn't a dream. I could see that from the footprints.

There they were again, the same huge footprints I'd seen the day before. They went all around the house, down to the garden, and then up to the root cellar. I could see my own smaller footprints. I saw other prints, too, tiny animal prints I didn't recognize.

I knelt down in front of the opening. Even though it was morning the opening was still black because the cellar was underground. Suddenly it got even darker.

Not again! I thought, feeling my knees start to tremble. I looked back. But it was just a cloud that had come over the sun and hid the light for a moment.

Hey, Andy, you're really freaking out, I told myself. Take it easy.

I waited for the cloud to pass so that the sun could come out again. Then I turned back and crawled a little inside the cellar. I stared.

It was a raccoon. Its throat was slashed and it lay in a pool of blood. Its mouth was open in the scream that I'd heard last night. Its eyes were open, too, and they looked at me with fear and horror.

I crouched at the opening to the root cellar, my heart started to beat like a drum. I stared at the terror in those small, black eyes.

I'd seen small animals dead in the forests before, but never like this. Everybody knew that raccoons were strong fighters, even against big animals. But this one never had a chance. Whatever killed it wasn't a fox, it wasn't even a bear. I wished I knew *what* it was.

"Meow!"

I jumped and hit my head against the rocks at the opening to the cellar.

It was Dutch, the small black cat that belonged to our neighbor, Mrs. Henderson. Dutch had smelled the raccoon and was now trying to get inside the root cellar. I picked him up and held him in my hands.

"There you are," a voice came from behind us. It was Mrs. Henderson. She lived in the house next to ours with Dutch the cat and a dog named Blake. "I let Dutch out and he immediately ran over to your house, Andy," she said. "He's been meowing and carrying on all night and all this morning."

"I think I know the reason, Mrs. Henderson," I told her. "It's right over there." I pointed to the dead raccoon in the root cellar. Dutch meowed again and made a move to get over there, but I held him tight.

Mrs. Henderson peered inside and then quickly took a step backwards. She looked white, as if she'd seen a ghost.

"Do you know what animal did that, Mrs. Henderson?" I asked her.

"No, Andy, I don't," she said. "Maybe it was a fox." She didn't look too well when she said that, as if she was suddenly sick.

"It looks to me like that animal was a lot bigger than a fox, Mrs. Henderson," I told her.

She wouldn't look me in the eye. Instead she looked up at Hunter Ridge. "I don't know what else it could be," she said. Her voice was shaking. "We don't have real big animals here, you know."

"Are you sure, Mrs. Henderson?"

"Of course I'm sure, Andy."

But she still didn't look straight at me. Instead she took Dutch out of my hands.

"Come on, Dutch," she said. "We're going home. And you're *staying* home. You're not going out any more!" She turned around so fast that her jacket caught on a bush nearby. But she pulled it off and started walking away quickly.

"Mrs. Henderson, it's faster to your house if you go across the ridge rather than down to the road," I yelled.

At first she didn't answer. But she kept on going towards the road and when she reached it, she finally turned around.

"If I were you, Andy, I wouldn't go across that ridge," she yelled. I could tell from her voice that she was frightened. "You hear me, Andy? Whatever you do, don't go up that ridge. Tell your parents I said so."

"Why not, Mrs. Henderson?" I yelled back.

"Just do what I say, Andy. I'm telling you this for your own good. Stay around the house. Don't go up there, you hear me? Don't go up there!"

4

Shades shook her head. "I don't understand it, Andy. I just don't understand it."

We were standing over the grave of the dead raccoon.

Shades had come over for a visit just as we'd finished supper. There was still a lot of light so

I showed her the dead raccoon. Together we dug a small grave for it behind our house. I also told Shades everything that happened last night, plus my meeting with Mrs. Henderson and Dutch that morning.

"Are you sure it's always stayed up in the hills?" I asked her.

"Always," she said. She had a catcher's mitt in one hand and a baseball in the other. I'd heard she was the best pitcher *and* the best catcher in the class. "It's always stayed up at the burial grounds by the Cave of the Dead. Nobody's ever seen it close to people's homes." She looked back at our house and the root cellar and shook her head. "The question is, why is it coming down now? And why to *your* house?" She took off her sunglasses and started chewing on one of its ends, thinking hard.

"There's only one way to find out, Shades."

"What's that?"

"We have to go up there and find out."

She almost threw the baseball at me. "Are you nuts?" she said. "It isn't bad enough the White Phantom is coming down here, you want to go up there?"

"You yourself said there's something crazy

going on up there."

"That doesn't mean we have to *do* something crazy!"

"What's the matter," I said, "are you afraid?"

I knew that would get to her. She stood up tall and looked me squarely in the eye. "Who are you calling afraid?"

"I'm not calling anybody afraid. All I'm saying is that I'm going to go up there even if you're not. It's time I went over there and took a look at this Cave of the Dead."

Her eyes got twice as big. "The Cave of the Dead! Nobody goes inside the Cave of the Dead, nobody. The Phantom guards it."

"I'm going anyway," I told her. "After all, it's only fair. The Phantom paid me a visit at my home last night. Why shouldn't I pay him a visit at his home?"

Shades opened her mouth to say something and then closed it again.

"Anyway," I said, "I'm going now before it gets too dark. You coming?"

She started shaking her head to say no, then stopped. "I'm coming," she groaned, and put her sunglasses back on.

"You're a pal!" I told her with a big smile.

"And you're nuts," she said right back. "Something tells me we're going to be real sorry before this day's over."

We went up the ridge, Shades leading. She knew all the paths and turns on the ridge. They were hidden by the leaves and trees, but Shades knew the way. I was lucky she was along.

But I could tell she was nervous. And she wasn't alone. According to my watch we should have had plenty of sunlight left, but I hadn't counted on the clouds that came up over the horizon and made the sky gray. They hid the sun and everything looked darker than usual. I must have looked up at the sky a lot because when we reached a turn onto a path Shades stopped. The path was going up to the hills. Immediately I guessed this was where she had seen the White Phantom one night.

"Are you sure you want to go on?" she said.

I wasn't sure at all. I hadn't thought it would be this dark already.

"Should we turn back?" Shades said.

"No," I told her. "We've come this far and nothing's happened yet."

I could tell that Shades thought that was pretty dumb. After all, we weren't at the Cave of the Dead yet. We weren't even near the burial grounds. But I had to say something just to keep my courage going.

We went up the path till it ended. Then we went up another path that started to climb. It went high up and twisted and turned around some big rocks. We were up in the hills now. I turned around and I could see the blue water of Hurley Creek down below, but everything else was hidden behind the trees. The path got narrower and narrower. It climbed up some more between a row of very tall trees and finally came to an end. We stopped.

In front of us was a gigantic plot of grass in the shape of a rectangle. It was surrounded by dense trees and bushes on three sides, so that it was almost impossible to get there except from the path where we stood. It was bare except for the grass and one enormous oak tree in the center. The tree was so big that its shadow covered almost the entire burial plot.

Shades pointed to something behind the tree. I looked and then I saw it. The Cave of the Dead.

From where we stood, it looked like a big

opening in the rocks. Behind it the hill went up even higher, so I knew for sure the cave must go deep underground.

Shades was about to step across the grass when I stopped her.

"Look who's scared now," she whispered.

"I'm not scared," I told her. Inside I knew that wasn't completely true. "My dad says we shouldn't walk on the burial plot with disrespect." I was whispering, too.

She let me go ahead and she walked behind me. We walked around the grass, along the trees. As we neared the cave, I looked at the gigantic oak in the middle. It had an opening in the bottom. I pointed it out to Shades.

"That's one of the biggest trees around," she whispered. "It's hollow inside and you can crawl in. I heard there's enough space in there for a football linebacker."

But as soon as we got to the cave, we forgot about the tree. The opening was very large. It looked like a big black hole in the rocks. We peered inside.

"It's too dark," Shades said. "I can't see anything. Let's go home."

"I brought a flashlight," I told her. She didn't

look too happy.

We took a few steps inside and stopped. Behind us the clouds had made the sky totally dark, even though it was not yet twilight. We both knew what that meant. The White Phantom would be coming soon. We didn't have much time.

I shone the flashlight all around. It was cool and wet inside the cave. There was dark moss on the wet rocks.

"Do you see anything?" Shades whispered. I practically jumped, she was so close.

"No," I whispered back. "Come on."

The ground was hard and full of pebbles. The ceiling got higher as we walked deeper and deeper inside. The cave turned, and we turned with it. Immediately all the light from the outside disappeared. Now we had only the flashlight, nothing else. I held it tight. The last thing I wanted to happen here was to be stuck without a light.

But even the flashlight didn't help. The hairs on the back of my neck were standing on edge, like antennas. Someone—something— was watching us.

I looked all around. I shone the flashlight everywhere. There were big boulders on the sides and I wondered if something could be hiding behind them. Nothing showed. But I knew we were being watched. And followed.

Suddenly Shades gripped my arm.

"What is it?" I asked.

"Can't you hear it?" she whispered back.

I listened hard. At first I couldn't hear a thing. But the next minute I did.

"It sounds like a soft hum," I said to her.

She nodded. We went in some more. The hum continued. In fact, it was getting louder and louder. Soon we could hear it clearly. I stopped still. So did Shades.

It was no longer a hum. It was a voice, low and slow. And it was calling my name: "An-dy! An-dy!"

We looked at each other. "It knows you!" Shades whispered. Her brown eyes were huge and scared. "It knows you're here!"

"An-dy, come! An-dy, come!"

"Let's get out of here, Andy!" Shades said. She was holding on to my hand. "It knows you. It wants something from you. I'm scared. Let's go!" She was pulling me away, back to the opening of the cave that by now was far behind us.

I was scared, too. The voice kept on saying my

name, louder and louder: "An-dy! An-dy, come!"

I closed my eyes. For a minute I didn't know what to do. I remembered the look of fear in Mrs. Henderson's eyes that morning. I remembered what Shades had said, that nobody ever leaves the Cave of the Dead alive. My hand came up to my neck and I could feel the black beads around it. What would the great Mohawk warrior have done if he were in my place?

"I'm going on," I told Shades. "I have to see what it is. I have to see what it wants."

"It wants to kill you, Andy," she said to me. "It wants to kill both of us. Let's get out of here while we still can."

"You leave if you want to," I said. "I have to go on."

"Then I'm going with you," she said.

We went on, step after step into that deep darkness. The light of the flashlight showed wet limestone over our heads. I thought of the Indians who came in here to die when they knew it was their time. It's not our time, Shades's or mine, I thought. Not yet, anyway.

Just as I was thinking that, a loud scream echoed all around us. I whirled around. It was Shades screaming. She screamed again and again. Her hand rose, shaking, and pointed behind me.

I turned around. The flashlight beam shone on the ground. I raised it higher. In front of us were two openings, one to the right and one to the left. And in between them, on a rocky ledge high above the openings, staring at us with its lifeless eyes and a deadly grin, was a human skull.

5

Shades couldn't stop screaming. My own hands shook so badly that I dropped the flashlight. It got completely dark and that made her scream some more. I picked it up and managed to turn the light back on and she finally stopped.

"I told you we shouldn't come here, I told you, I told you!"

"It's just a skull, Shades." I was trying to play it cool for her sake, but deep inside I was completely terrified.

"What do you mean, just a skull!"

"It's been dead a long time. Ages!"

"How do you know?"

"You were the one who told me that this was the place where the warriors came to die. That was a long time ago!"

I looked at it again with the beam of my flashlight. I'd never seen a skull before. It had holes for eyes so I knew it couldn't see us, but those empty holes stared at us as if they could. Its mouth was an empty hole, too, but it looked as if it were grinning.

I shone the flashlight on the two openings beneath the skull, one going right and one going left.

"Oh, Andy," Shades said, "that skull's up there for a reason. It's there to warn us away."

"We've come this far, Shades," I said. "Let's not leave now just because of some skull."

"I think that running into somebody's skull in the Cave of the Dead is a pretty good reason to leave," she told me. "Besides, which way do we go now?"

I looked at the openings. They were both dark. I looked at the skull again. Beneath it was a large rock that was shaped almost like a wheel. I'd never seen a rock in that shape before.

I pointed to the right. "Let's go that way."

"Why?"

"You want to go to the left and I'll go to the right?"

"No way I'm going alone," Shades said, pretty annoyed by now. "Besides, you're the one with the flashlight."

That made us both laugh a little.

Then together we went through the opening on the right.

The cave here was a lot narrower. It was like a tunnel that turned and twisted the longer we walked. After a few minutes Shades said, "Andy, do you notice something?"

I looked around. "What is it?"

"The voice is getting quieter," she said.

Shades was right. I'd stopped paying attention to the voice. It hadn't stopped calling my name even when we stood in front of the skull. I could still hear it even now, "An-dy! An-dy, come!" But Shades was right. It was quieter now. And the deeper we walked, the quieter the voice got.

Shades sighed in relief. I felt a little better, too. It was getting quieter all the time. That meant that we were getting farther and farther away from it, or wherever it came from. Soon I could hardly hear my name anymore. It was like the whisper that we'd first heard when we were in the entrance of the cave. Then it turned silent. Completely silent.

I looked over my shoulder at Shades and she looked back at me. She didn't feel so good anymore. Neither did I. Before, when the voice was calling me, we were pretty scared. But we'd gotten used to it after a few minutes. Now it was suddenly very quiet and that felt a lot scarier. I could feel Shades getting closer to me. I could hear her footsteps on the hard ground.

"Stop making so much noise," I whispered back to her.

"Who's making noise?"

"You are. You're walking so loud."

And then I stopped short. Shades ran straight into me. "What are—" she started saying but I motioned her to be quiet.

Shades had stopped walking and I'd stopped walking. But something else hadn't. I could hear the slow footsteps. They weren't ours. Shades could hear them, too. She stopped breathing.

"It's up ahead of us," she whispered nervously into my ear.

I listened hard. She was right. I listened some more. It was moving a little faster now, the pitter-patter of feet. And then I knew. I remembered. Those weren't human feet, they were something else, something I'd heard in the middle of the night—

"Shades," I whispered aloud, looking at her, "I know what it is. I heard it last night. It's the—"

"White Phantom!"

I don't know which of us said it. All I know is that we both turned and ran for our lives.

We ran and ran, and the White Phantom ran behind us. We ran as fast as we could, Shades leading the way. She ran so fast she could have set a record. But even Shades wasn't running as fast as the White Phantom. It was chasing us now, all right. It had caught our smell, it knew we were in the cave, and it was coming after us.

"Hurry, Andy, hurry!" Shades yelled over her shoulder. "We're almost at the opening. Hurry!"

I was breathing so hard I thought my lungs would collapse. I don't think I ever ran so fast in all my life. Sure enough, there was the opening where we'd seen the skull. Shades ran straight through it and then ran on in the direction of the opening to the cave. But I got an idea.

"Shades!"

I could see she didn't want to stop, but she

did. I didn't wait for her. I got on the other side of the big rock that looked like a wheel and started pushing it.

"What are you doing?" she yelled. "Come quick! It's after us!"

"I'm going to move the rock. It'll block the opening. The Phantom won't be able to get out!"

"Are you crazy?" she yelled again. "It's a spirit. It can go anywhere it wants!"

But I pushed and pushed the rock, and slowly I could feel it move toward the opening. Shades hurried over to me and pushed, too.

I could hear the loud breath of the Phantom. "It's coming, Shades!" I yelled. "Push hard!"

Now the rock was really moving. It began to cover the opening. A little more, and a little more. I kept pushing.

"It's coming!" Shades cried out, and started to run again.

I gave the rock one more heave and it moved against the opening, covering it flat.

"Come on!" Shades yelled over her shoulder.

But I stayed by the rock. There was a small space between it and the wall, and I looked through it.

I could hear the fast footsteps now and the

hot, loud breath. And then what looked like a gigantic light came running up from the dark caverns of the cave. But as it got closer it was my turn to scream. Because that big light was not a light, it was a tremendous white head, as white as snow and bigger than any animal that ever lived. Its eyes were burning red and they stared straight at me even though I was hidden by the rock. Its mouth was open. It was huge and black, but I could see its white fangs, as long and sharp as knives. When it saw the rock, it snarled so loudly my eardrums nearly cracked. The snarl echoed and echoed in the cave, louder and louder each time.

I flew after Shades.

"Hurry, Andy!" she yelled, way ahead of me.

Would it get through the rock, I wondered even as I was running. Not if it's a regular animal, but if it's a spirit then nothing will stop it! Nothing!

As I ran, I could hear the snarling behind the rock. I looked over my shoulder. So far the rock was holding. But the noise grew louder and louder. And then it happened. The walls around us began to tremble, as if there was an earthquake. The earth under our feet began to shake, and I could feel small stones falling from the ceiling of the cave.

"Run, Andy! We're almost out!" Shades yelled.

Ahead of her was the opening to the cave. She ran through it but I was still behind her.

The snarling behind me was like thunder. The Cave of the Dead was shivering and shaking, stones falling down the walls like an avalanche. Was it going to come crashing all around me and bury me alive?

Suddenly there was an explosion. Stones hit my back. I looked over my shoulder and all I could see was a huge light once again, the sound of footsteps, and a growl of rage.

Once again, it was coming after me.

But now I was through the opening. There were stars above me, a clear night sky. "Shades!" I yelled. "Shades! Where are you?"

"Here, in the tree!" she yelled back. "Come inside the tree!"

I didn't waste one second. I ran to the big oak in the middle of the burial grounds. Behind me I heard the White Phantom.

"It's right behind you, Andy! Hurry!"

Ahead of me was the small opening to the tree. I slid into it feet first, as if I were running to third base. My feet got in, then my legs. Shades pulled in the rest of me till my head was now inside, also.

Then she looked down and screamed. I looked down, too.

Two gigantic red eyes stared through the opening. They looked straight at us, never blinking once.

We stayed all night inside the oak tree by the Cave of the Dead. All night we heard the snarls and growls of the White Phantom. Shades and I huddled close together. When I was scared I touched the black beads around my neck. Finally we fell asleep. When we woke up it was morning and the Phantom was not there. When I got home, I told my parents I had stayed over with Shades. But I didn't say where.

After school Shades said she wanted us to visit somebody who lived not far from her house. His name was Jack Fire Keeper Michel, she said, and he was a shaman.

"He's a Seneca shaman," Shades said. "He's a

very wise man. Maybe he can help us."

We walked to a cabin in the woods not far from Shades's house. When Shades knocked on the door a thin man with long black hair and many wrinkles opened it. He looked very old. But he smiled when he saw Shades and told us to come inside.

I really liked his home. It wasn't big like our house; in fact, the cabin was only one room. But the room was big and neat. There were lots of blankets around the fireplace and that's where he told us to sit. On the wooden wall above the fireplace hung a wampum belt with purple beads and a headdress with beautiful, colorful feathers.

But the shaman himself wore just blue jeans and a flannel shirt. I was a little disappointed till I noticed that the top buttons of the shirt were open, and he was wearing a chain of beads that looked a little like mine. Only those beads were a lot of different colors, and there were so many of them that they covered his chest.

Then I noticed that he was staring at my chain of beads, too. "Where did you get those black beads?" he asked me.

I explained about the Mohawk warrior and

how our family had had the beads for generations. "It was my turn to get them, because last month I was just 12."

"Black beads are very powerful," he said. His eyes were very dark, almost as black as my beads.

"Is a shaman like a medicine man?" I asked him. "Can you do great magic?"

He smiled slowly. Though he was very old he sat cross-legged on the blankets on the floor. "I can do small magic," he said. "Not great magic. You, Andrew Baker, can do small magic, too. The black beads you are wearing are much more powerful than I am."

"Really?"

"I do not wear the black beads. Black beads are worn only by great warriors."

"Can they help us against the White Phantom?" Shades asked.

"Why do you wish for help against the White Phantom?" the shaman asked. "Where did you see the White Phantom?"

"We saw it in the Cave of the Dead. We went there yesterday," I told him.

The shaman's face changed immediately. "You were *inside* the Cave of the Dead?" He looked first at Shades, then at me. Then he looked at me a long time. "No one returns alive from the Cave of the Dead."

"We did," told him.

He looked at me again strangely, and then his eyes came down to the beads around my neck. "You came back because they protected you," he told me. "These beads once belonged to a great warrior. Even the Phantom respects black beads. Say a prayer of thanks to your Mohawk ancestor. Without the beads you would not be sitting here now."

I looked at Shades and she looked at me.

"Do you ever touch the beads?" the shaman asked.

"No," I said. "I usually just wear them. Except—" I stared at him. I couldn't go on.

"Except when you're frightened, Andrew Baker?"

I nodded. How did he know?

"Last night, when we hid inside the tree and the Phantom was outside trying to come in, I touched the beads because I was afraid. And the night before that when the Phantom came to the house and was right behind me I touched the beads, too, because I was scared."

Again the shaman's face changed. His black eyes were full of amazement. "The Phantom came to your house?" he asked me.

"It was outside our root cellar right in back of the house. I heard a scream and went over to investigate, and it came up right behind me. I was so terrified I couldn't look. I just saw its shadow. That's when I touched the black beads."

The shaman looked at the black beads, saying nothing. But there was a worried look in his eyes

"Why is the White Phantom doing this, Mr. Michel?" Shades asked. "It never left Hunter Ridge before. Why is it coming down to Andy's house?"

"It is coming down to Andy's house because it is haunting Andy."

I stared at him. "It's haunting *me*? Why?"

The shaman pointed to the beads around my neck. "Because of them," he said.

I touched the black beads. They were warm against my skin.

He nodded quietly. "The beads protect you, Andrew Baker. But they also attract the White Phantom. It knows you have them, and it will never leave you alone."

I got chills when he said that. I wished I had

a sweater with me. "It will never leave me alone!" Both the shaman and Shades were looking at the beads around my neck. I could feel them on my skin as I'd never felt them before. My mouth was dry and it was hard for me to talk. "Why? What does it want from me?"

The shaman shook his head. "I don't know what it wants. But this I do know." He raised his hand and pointed at the black beads. "You, Andrew Baker, have the black beads around your neck. You have a mission to fulfill. The Phantom will not leave you until you fulfill that mission."

"What mission is that?" I asked him.

He said nothing.

"How can I fulfill a mission if I don't know what it is?"

The shaman didn't say anything for a long time. He just looked at the black beads in silence for several minutes, and then he said, "Find something that belongs to us."

7

"There's going to be a thunderstorm tonight," Mom said. "I can smell it."

She was right. The clouds from the day before were back. They covered the sky and hung low. We were going to get rain. And thunder and lightning, too, by the looks of it.

"You're not eating, Andy," Mom said. "Are you worried about that storm?"

"Of course not," I told her, and just to show her I wasn't, I started quickly eating my mashed potatoes.

But it was hard for me to eat. I wasn't worried about the storm, I was worried about the White Phantom. It had come down to the house every night since we moved here. It was going to come again tonight.

What am I going to do, I wondered. Every time I closed my eyes I could see the shadow that came up behind me when I'd crouched by the root cellar in back of the house. And when I didn't see that, I saw the two huge red eyes looking up at Shades and me through the opening in the giant oak tree.

My hand started shaking and I held the fork real tight. Otherwise the mashed potatoes would have gone flying across the room. The shaman's words came back to me over and over again. "You, Andrew Baker, have the black beads around your neck. You have a mission to fulfill." And then he'd added, "Find something that belongs to us."

What did that mean? And what was the White Phantom going to do tonight?

"Mom, Dad," I said, putting my mashed potatoes down. "What belonged to the Seneca Indians that they lost?"

Mom looked up from her food. Then she looked at Dad. "The only thing I can think of is the land. All the American Indians lost lands when the white settlers came. You know that, Andy."

"What about the burial grounds on top of the ridge?" I asked. "Don't those belong to them?"

"Yes and no," Dad said. He buttered a piece of bread. "You see, Andy, the Seneca Indians got those lands because that's where they buried their dead. That means nobody is allowed to build homes there or live there. The trouble is, they lost the deeds to those lands."

"What are deeds?" I asked.

"Deeds are papers that show something belongs to you," Mom explained. "We have a deed to this house that proves we own it."

"And the Senecas had the deeds to the burial

grounds. The trouble is, those deeds disappeared when the last Seneca chief, John White Wind Gray, disappeared."

"What happened to him, Dad?"

"Nobody knows. He disappeared about five years ago. And since the chief always had the deeds in his possession, when Chief White Wind disappeared, the deeds disappeared, too."

"But don't people know that the Indians own those lands?"

"Many people know it. But knowing it is one thing and proving it is something else. Sometimes somebody tries to take that land. So far nobody has succeeded, but if those deeds aren't found, it's just a matter of time before somebody will. And then the Indians will lose it forever. So you see, those deeds are very important."

"Why all this sudden interest in Seneca Indians and burial grounds?" Mom asked me. "Is that something you're learning in school?"

I didn't say anything. We finished dinner quickly. I did some homework while Mom and Dad unpacked more things from our move. Pretty soon I was tired because I hadn't slept much the night before. But as tired as I was, I was afraid to fall asleep. A voice inside kept on telling me that something was going to happen, that the White Phantom was going to come back.

As I fell asleep, I decided one thing. Whatever happened this time, I wasn't going to leave the house. No matter what you see or what you hear, I told myself, nothing terrible can happen if you don't leave the house.

Thunder woke me up.

Only I never heard thunder this loud before. I opened my eyes, and just as I did a bright streak flashed across the room and made it as light as day.

The thunder crashed again. I could hear the rain pouring and splashing outside. It beat so hard against the windowpanes it could have broken them. Mom had shut the windows before I went to bed because she said it was going to storm. But even she didn't think it was going to be like this, because if she had, she would have shut all of them all the way. But the one right by my bed was open at the very bottom, just a few inches. The thunder kept crashing and crashing.

Somebody whispered, "Andy!"

I looked around. The lightning flashed again. There was nobody in the room.

"Andy!"

My heart started beating loudly. It was a man's voice and it was whispering to me. But it wasn't Dad.

"Andy!"

I clutched the sheet tight over my body. What did the shaman say? "It's coming to Andy's house because it's haunting Andy."

"Go away!" I said. But I felt stupid talking to the empty, dark air in the room.

"Andy, come!"

The words from the Cave of the Dead! Only this time it was a whisper, not a loud, echoing cry. And the whisper was coming through the window.

No, I said to myself. I'm not going. I'm not going. I'm not leaving the house.

If I went out of the house, I might never come home again.

"Andy!"

Maybe I can just look out the window, I thought. I don't have to go out. I can just look out the window.

Thunder struck again.

I didn't get out of bed. Instead I got up on my knees and shuffled across the bed to the window. I looked out.

At first I couldn't see anything. Rain was still smashing hard against the glass.

I should close the window completely, I thought; otherwise the bed will get drenched. Suddenly there was a tremendous flash of lightning and an explosion.

It must have hit a tree out in back because I heard a gigantic c-r-r-r-ack and something came crashing down on the ground. But I didn't pay attention. Because in the lightning I saw something that made the hair on the back of my neck stand up, and I had to hold on to the windowsill hard to stop from shaking.

In the flash of lightning I could see a man. He was standing right outside my window, not four feet away. I could have put my hand out to touch him. He had long black hair like the shaman. But he was younger and taller and he wore yellow buckskin pants and a jacket, just as Indians did long ago. On his head he wore the feather headdress that I'd seen in the shaman's cabin.

He stared straight at me.

In an instant the darkness was back and I couldn't see him. My knees trembled so badly I almost fell on the bed. But I held on to the windowsill, staring hard out the window. I had to wait for the next lightning flash. I had to make sure I didn't imagine it.

The lightning came and lit up our backyard and the ridge behind it like daylight. And in the light I saw him again, still standing on the other side of the window, still staring straight at me. And this time I saw something else, too.

Even though it rained like crazy, the man was completely dry.

And he was motioning to me. His arm came towards me and motioned for me to come.

Come to him.

In the morning I checked all around the house, especially by my bedroom window. The only sign of the storm was the fallen maple tree which was hit by lightning. The ground was muddy but there were no footprints anywhere. And there wasn't even a trace of footprints outside my window where the man had stood last night, motioning to me to come.

Right after school I went out looking for Shades, but she was pitching a baseball game in the schoolyard, wearing her red L.A. Dodger baseball cap. She waved to me and I waved back. But this time I didn't wait for her. I knew what I wanted to do, and I wasn't sure she'd want to do it with me.

I was going back to the Cave of the Dead.

The afternoon was bright and sunny as I walked up the ridge alone. I felt funny going up there without Shades. She not only knew her way around these hills better than anybody else, she was also my best friend. But the White Phantom had come after me, not after her. It wanted something from me because I wore the black beads. It was better to go there alone.

The sun was over Hurley Creek. There were a couple of hours left before it was going to set. The White Phantom never came out before sunset, Shades always said. That meant I had time to go to the Cave and come out again before the Phantom came out. At least, I hoped I did. Every time I thought of the White Phantom chasing me inside the cave, its huge white teeth in the open black mouth, the red eyes and the monstrous white head, I knew I didn't dare face that spirit again. I'd already seen it twice, once behind the root cellar and once in the Cave of the Dead.

Both times it had opened its jaws and would have killed me if not for the black beads.

The next time would be the third time. Three strikes and I'd be out.

I knew there had better not be a third time.

I went up the path that led to the burial grounds. I came to the long, high plot of grass with the giant oak in the middle. Behind the oak was the black opening to the Cave of the Dead. Shades and I had run from the cave to the big oak that night and crawled in. The oak saved our lives. That, and the black beads.

I walked around the plot of grass just as we did last time, but things felt funny already. Once again, I was being watched. I knew it. I looked all around. The plot was out in the open air. There was nothing to see. But I felt for sure that somebody—something—was following every move I made. I looked at the trees in the forest and they looked back. Nothing. But the skin on the back of my neck was tingling. Somebody was looking at me back there. Who was it?

I stood in front of the the Cave of the Dead. This is it, I thought. I thought of the Indian warriors who used to come here to die many years ago. I said a silent prayer to them. I'm not coming in here to disturb you, I told them. I'm coming here because I've been called. Whatever happens, I promised, this will be the last time I visit the Cave of the Dead.

I felt the black beads inside my shirt. Then I went inside.

It turned a lot cooler as soon as I went in. I took a few steps. Something cold touched my back and I jumped and turned around. But it was just a drop of icy water that fell from the ceiling. Take it easy, Andy, I told myself. The beam of the flashlight showed that the rocks on the sides of the cave were big and wet.

But when I shone my flashlight on the ground there were no stones by my feet. That's funny, I thought. Where were the rocks that fell from the walls of the cave when Shades and I ran away from the Phantom? I remembered how the cave shook and how stones and gravel came rolling down all around us. But now there was nothing there. It was almost as if somebody with a gigantic broom had come afterwards and swept away all the stones and rocks, all the traces. The ground was as hard and neat as it had been the first time we went in.

I made a turn and went inside. It was very

dark and I thought of the afternoon sun outside. Shades was probably pitching a good game. She always did when she wore her red shades and her Dodgers cap. I wished she was here with me.

Ahead of me were the two openings that went deeper into the Cave, one going left and one going right. I took a deep breath and moved the flashlight higher. The skull was still there. I knew it would be, but it still gave me the shivers. The empty eye sockets looked at me just as before, the empty mouth grinned as if it knew something I didn't.

Maybe Shades was right, I thought to myself, shivering. Maybe the ancient Senecas put it up there as a warning for people to keep away. It sure would do the trick.

Then I moved the flashlight down, and I couldn't believe my eyes. The big wheel-shaped rock stood between the two doorways, just as it had when we first came. I stared hard at it. I knew I didn't imagine things. I knew I'd moved it to block the right opening when the White Phantom had chased after us two days before. But now it stood exactly where it was last time, as though it hadn't been moved in hundreds and hundreds of years!

Who's doing this, I wondered. What's going on here?

Again I felt as if I were being watched. Something was following me. Something knew I was here. I spun around quickly and shone the flashlight all around. But the cave was dark. Nothing moved. Silence.

I looked right, then I looked left. Both openings were completely dark. We'd gone right the last time and the White Phantom was there. This time I went to the left.

I went in deeper and deeper. There were lots of turns in the black tunnel. I tried to walk carefully in my flashlight beam, but I couldn't help bumping into rocks and walls. And then I stopped.

It was the whisper again. At first I could hardly hear it. Then it got a little louder, and a little louder again. But I didn't need to hear the words, I already knew what they were:

"An-dy! An-dy, come!"

It wasn't like the voice of last night. The voice last night was like a whisper in my ear, as if somebody were right in the room with me. This voice was getting louder and louder, and it came from deep inside the cave.

It knows I'm here, I thought. It's calling for me.

I stopped for a moment. What do I do now, I wondered. Should I go on?

I had to go on. I had to find where the voice was coming from.

The deeper I went into the cave, the louder it got. Soon it was thundering in my ears:

"An-dy! An-dy, come!"

I took one more turn in the tunnel. Then I came to a stop. I wasn't in a tunnel anymore. There were no more narrow walls, no more rocks to bump into. The voice was yelling now: "Andy! Andy!"

I waved the flashlight around me. I was in a cavern, a small room. The voice was coming from somewhere to the right. I tried to walk in the direction it came from.

"Andy! Andy, come!"

I waved the flashlight across the walls and then on the floor. Something lay on the floor straight ahead of me. I bent over it.

It was an old briefcase. It felt wet and worn under my hands. I couldn't open it right away because there were two straps hung over it. I picked up the handle. It felt light in my hand. I wondered what was in it.

As I handled it, my hand made the beam from the flashlight carom across the wall and then down, just a few feet from where I was standing. I looked and froze. I couldn't move. I couldn't breathe. I couldn't even scream.

The man I'd seen right outside my window last night lay only five feet away from me. I knew it was the man because he wore the same yellow buckskin pants and jacket, and had the feather headdress.

Only it wasn't the man, it was his skeleton.

I dropped the flashlight and the light went out. Something icy touched my neck and I screamed. It was pitch black. I couldn't see anything. I touched the back of my neck. It felt cold and wet. Another drop of icy water from the ceiling of the cave. I bent down and tried to find the flashlight. But my hand shook so hard and it was so dark I couldn't find it. Then I felt it near my foot. I picked it up and turned the beam on. It was working. I took a deep breath of relief and shone it on the bones at my feet.

It had a skull like the one at the entrance, only this skull had hair on it, long black hair below the feather headdress. It also had teeth that shone in the darkness. Its clothes were rotting away and through the holes I could see its gray bones.

But the clothes told me that it was he, the man who had called to me last night.

He must have been dead for years.

He was looking at me. The empty eye sockets were staring at me as though they were expecting me. The arm was stretched out towards me, one finger pointing.

"An-dy! An-dy!"

My hand trembled so hard that I had to clutch the flashlight tight; otherwise I would have dropped it again.

"An-dy! An-dy!"

I screamed once. Then I picked up the briefcase and ran.

I ran back the way I came, down the narrow tunnel. It twisted and turned. I bumped into walls and rocks, but I didn't care. I ran and ran and ran. I wanted to get out of there, away from the skeleton, away from the pointing finger, away from the voice that was saying my name over and over.

I ran to the passage where the two turns met. In my mind's eye I could see the sun outside, the darkening blue sky, the birds chirping in the late afternoon. I ran faster than ever before. Any minute now, I thought to myself as I ran. I'll run through the opening and then down to the front of the cave and out the entrance. And I'll never, ever, ever come back to the Cave of the Dead again.

I ran even harder now, following the beam of the flashlight. It fell on something straight in front of me but I ran toward it anyway.

I couldn't believe it. I couldn't believe it till I touched it with my own hands.

The doorway was blocked. Somebody—something—had pushed the wheel-shaped rock in front of the entryway, covering it completely.

I pushed hard against it. It didn't move.

I went crazy. I threw myself at the rock again and again. It didn't move an inch.

I touched the beads under my shirt, but I was so scared my shirt was wet with perspiration.

I was a prisoner inside the cave. And this time there was no way out.

I was cold. My clothes were wet.

I was sitting on the ground. It was damp, and I felt cold and dirty. I didn't know how much time had passed. Hours, maybe.

My flashlight beam was getting weaker. The battery was probably going. That meant that soon I would be in total darkness.

Don't think about that, I told myself. Think about how you can get out of here.

I thought hard. Before coming here I hadn't told anybody where I was going. I tried to figure out how long it might be before they thought to look for me here. My parents would call the police tonight when I didn't get back. They would start checking around, and Shades would tell them about the Cave of the Dead. That meant they might not get up here till tomorrow.

By then it would be too late. One minute after today's sunset would be too late.

"Andy!"

I opened my eyes.

"Andy!"

"Shades?"

"It's me, Andy."

I couldn't believe it. I jumped to my feet and went the rock. Sure enough, a small light shone through the small gap between the rock and the wall. The beam of a flashlight.

"Shades, what are you doing here?" I was never so happy to hear a human voice in my entire life.

"I followed you up here."

"You did what?"

"I saw you at the baseball game. I waved to you. I wanted you to wait, but you left. At the end of the game I looked for you, but you were gone. Nobody knew where you were. But *I* knew, so I came up here."

"Weren't you scared to come in here again?"

"Of course not," she said in a huff. "If you're not scared, why should I be?"

"Well, I'm really scared now, Shades," I told her. "I'm really, *really* scared now."

"What's this rock doing here, Andy? Wasn't this open last time?"

"It was open when I came in. But something pushed the rock against the door. Something doesn't want me to leave the cave." I swallowed. "Not alive, anyway."

"The White Phantom!" Shades whispered on the other side. "Listen, Andy, I'm going to try to move the rock. Wait here."

"There isn't much else I can do," I reminded her.

"Very funny," she said.

I could hear her take a deep breath, then another and another.

"It's not moving, Andy," she said. "I can't move it on my own."

"Listen, Shades, there's no time to lose." I started talking quickly. "You've got to go get help. Get my mom and dad, tell them what happened. Tell them to come up here quickly. Can you do that?"

"Sure. But I don't want to leave you alone."

"There's no choice. You're the only one who can get help. But you have to go *now*, Shades. You have to hurry!"

"Okay, I'm going. I'm running. I'll come back as fast as I can." She paused. "Andy, don't forget your black beads. The shaman said they'd protect you."

"Thanks for reminding me," I told her. "Now, go!" I heard her turn. "Wait, Shades. Tell me one thing. What time is it?"

"It's almost seven."

Almost seven. Sunset. I swallowed hard.

"Thanks, Shades. Now, run!"

I heard her footsteps. She ran all right. She was fast, too, the fastest runner in the class. If anybody could bring help quickly, it was Shades.

But would she bring it in time?

It was seven o'clock. That meant that the sun was setting, the skies were getting darker. The hour of the White Phantom was coming.

I leaned against the old briefcase. It smelled like mold. Suddenly I wondered what it was doing in the cave. I hadn't had the chance to think about it till now. Quickly I opened the straps. They were so worn they almost tore off.

There wasn't much power left in the battery, and the light from my flashlight was growing dim. I pointed the light inside and saw a big manila envelope.

Suddenly I had an idea. It was a crazy idea, and my hand trembled as I reached for the envelope and took it out. I opened it and pointed the light beam on the papers. It was getting real dark now, but in the small light I saw the word "DEED" in big capital letters. The other papers had "DEED" written on them, too. And there was a signature scrawled on the bottom of the last page and underneath were the words, "Governor, State of New York."

The deeds to the Seneca burial grounds. They were in my hands! They'd been lost for years, and now I had them!

My mind raced. If these were the deeds, I thought, then that man—that skeleton—was John White Wind Gray, the Seneca tribal chief who had disappeared! He'd come up here to die and he'd brought the papers with him.

My mind felt as if it were exploding. Quickly I put the papers back into the envelope and into the brief case. I needed to think things out, back to the first day when I saw the footprints above our house. The shadow that crept behind me when I looked into the root cellar. The voice that called me in the cave. The visit to the shaman. What did he say? "Find something that belongs to us." The man who stood outside motioning to me to come. That was the chief. He wanted me to find him. He wanted me to find the—

Did something move? My blood froze. I listened hard. No, nothing. Yes, there was something. There was definitely something. I swallowed hard. I was thirsty—badly, badly thirsty, but it didn't matter. Nothing mattered now. Was it a whisper? Was it the voice calling me? No, it was no whisper.

My body turned to ice. It was footsteps.

I took a deep breath. I tried to relax. But it was too late to relax, too late for anything. The footsteps were slow now, soft and slow, but it was just a question of time before—

Now they were faster. Yes, they were definitely faster. I could hear them deep in the caverns of the cave, deep down under, wherever it stayed in the daytime hours. The sun had set, and it was coming out. The White Phantom.

And now it started to run. It must have caught my scent; it knew I was here in the Cave of the Dead, which nobody must leave alive. It was coming after me. It was coming—

My light went out. It was dark, but only for a minute. I leaned back against the rocks of the cave, clutching the briefcase against my chest. There was light again, but not from the flashlight. It was from the other direction, the direction of the room where I'd found the skeleton. And it wasn't just a light. It was the monstrous spirit with the huge white head, as white as the moon. The White Phantom. It was heading this way. It was finally coming for me.

Shades would be too late. They would all be too late. By the time they came I'd—

The growling filled the cavern and made echo after echo. It got louder and louder. It was getting closer.

The Phantom knew I was here. It was in a rage.

My hand came up to the black beads. "They will protect you," the shaman had said.

But the Phantom was coming. The light in the tunnel was getting brighter and brighter. Any second now, any second—

It saw me. And I saw it. I saw the red eyes, the huge tongue dangling from the black open mouth, the long, cruel, white teeth. It saw me. The echoes of its running feet filled the cave. The white head was almost on top of me. It opened its mouth wide. I could feel its hot breath all around me. I saw the large black open mouth, the knifelike teeth—

I screamed once. Then everything turned black.

10

It felt as if I were sailing on a boat, warm and comfortable. I opened my eyes. I was under a blanket and there were stars. Dad's face was right above mine.

"Dad?"

"Don't say anything, Andrew," he said. "We're taking you home."

I must have fallen asleep after that, because the next time I opened my eyes I was in my bed. Shades was sitting on the floor next to me. She wasn't wearing her sunglasses.

"Hi, Andy," she said with a big grin.

"How did I get here?" I asked her.

"Your mom says you shouldn't talk, she says you've been through too much. Of course, she doesn't know *how* much."

We both grinned at each other. Then she whispered. "What happened?"

"I don't know," I told her.

"When we moved the rock away, we found you unconscious."

"I think I passed out."

She looked at me. "Did the White Phantom

come for you?"

I nodded.

"Do you remember anything?"

"I remember touching the black beads around my neck," I told her, and I now touched them just to make sure they were there where they were supposed to be. "And I was holding this brief-case—what happened to the briefcase?"

"Your dad gave it to Mr. Michel. You should have seen his eyes when he heard what was in it." She leaned toward me. "That's what saved you, Andy. The lost deeds and the black beads. It was just as the shaman said. You found something that belonged to them. The White Phantom couldn't touch you after that. I don't think it's going to come here and bother you any more."

"You know what I think, Shades?" I said. "I don't think it's going to bother anybody any more. I think it's going to disappear."

"What makes you say that?"

"I think the White Phantom also had its mission. It had to protect the burial grounds from strangers. And it had to protect the deeds that were in the cave."

"So now that you found them there's no need for the Phantom," Shades said. "I see what you mean." Then she grinned again. "Aren't you going to miss it, Andy?"

I looked at the window over my bed. "No," I said, "I'm not going to miss it. For one thing, I'm finally going to get a good night's sleep." I turned over to the side. The events of the last few days started to whirl in my mind. I felt the fear, the terror, the enormous sense of relief and safety all over again.

"Maybe one day it'll come back," Shades continued. She kept on talking, but I'd stopped listening. I was fast asleep.

NIGHTMARE NEIGHBORS

by Sandra Shictman

1

T oday's the day!" I told myself, springing
out of bed. Tryout day for the school
band. I went to the window and pulled
up the shade. The brightness of the sun's rays
nearly blinded me. I thought of what my dad always said. A sunny day is a good sign that the
day will go well.

Still in my bare feet, I padded over to the
dresser and took my clarinet out of its case.
Quickly, I ran through the notes of the song I'd

been practicing for two weeks, *Sunset Dreams*. I played the whole thing through without a single mistake. I smiled to myself. By three o'clock today, I thought, I'll be back in the school band. I was sure of it.

When I headed downstairs, I heard my baby sister crying in her crib. That's funny, I thought. Mom always takes Amy down and feeds her before my dad and I get up. I went into her room and put a rattle into her hand. That calmed her. She smiled and said "Goo! Goo!" to me a couple of times. I suppose that was her way of saying "Thank you." But why had Mom left her alone upstairs?

Mom was in the kitchen frying eggs. Her back was turned to me. She had a small TV playing on the counter nearby. The sound was turned off. I said, "Good morning" and plopped myself into a chair.

"Sunny-side up eggs OK?" Mom asked without turning around.

"Sure, OK," I said. I glanced at the TV set, where a man was pointing to a weather map, probably telling everyone that it was going to be another perfect day for outdoor activities. Anyone could see that just by looking out the window, I thought. Something on the counter in front of the TV caught my eye. I got up to take a closer look. It was a small puddle of yellow-green liquid.

"What's that?" I asked Mom, pointing to the yucky-looking mess.

"Don't worry about it," she said, slipping my eggs onto a plate. She turned to me. "Here. Eat this before it gets cold. I'll clean that up later."

I couldn't believe what she said. My mother, who always told me to wash my hands, who always kept the house spotless, was telling me she'd clean up something later! Then I saw her face. Her forehead had a Band-Aid across it. "Did you fall, Mom?" I asked, "or bump your head against something?"

Mom's hand went to her forehead. "I don't think so," she said. "I don't know how I got this."

That's strange, I thought, taking my plate to the table. I always knew exactly how I got every cut and bruise.

I looked down at my eggs. The yolks were sort of yellow-green, like the stuff on the counter. I took a sniff. They smelled like regular eggs. Maybe Mom bought them at the health food store. They had lots of weird things there. Or did she have more of the stuff on the counter? "Did you mix in some of that gook from the counter with my eggs?" I asked Mom.

"Don't get smart with me, young man," Mom said. "There's nothing wrong with those eggs. Now eat your breakfast. You don't want to be late for school."

"Only kidding, Mom," I said, digging in. They tasted OK. What was wrong with Mom today? What happened to her sense of humor? I gulped down the eggs and put the plate in the sink when I was finished. I noticed that the gook was still on the counter. Mom was slowing down, I thought. Ordinarily, she'd have that stuff cleaned up a minute after she first saw it.

I went upstairs. My baby sister was still playing with her rattle. "Hey, princess," I said to her. My dad calls her that, so I do, too. "What's that I smell? Mommy will come up soon and change your diaper." Was what was in her diaper the same yellow-green color as the blob on the kitchen counter? It sure smelled like it should be, I told myself.

My hair was still damp from the shower, so I turned on the blow dryer and dried my hair.

I rubbed my stomach. Suddenly, I wasn't feeling very good. Maybe those eggs really *were* bad. Or maybe it's just that I'm a little nervous about the band tryout, I thought, trying not to pay attention to the ache in my stomach. Instead, I concentrated on my hair. I wished that it was any color but red. I sure stood out in school. I was the only kid in the whole school who had bright red hair.

By the time I went back to my room for my clarinet and backpack, my stomach was really hurting. There had to have been something wrong with those eggs I ate, after all. I didn't know what to do. I didn't really want to miss school today. Besides, Mom never let me stay home unless I had a fever. But I really felt terrible. And, besides, it was Mom's fault I had a stomach ache. She made me eat those eggs. I put my stuff back on the desk and went downstairs.

Mom was still in the kitchen. "Mom," I said. "I don't feel very good. My stomach hurts." I thought about trying to convince her. But I didn't have to.

"Go upstairs and lie down for awhile," she said. "I'll call Susan and tell her you won't be walking to school with her today. If you feel better, you can go in this afternoon. I'll write a note for you to give to your teacher."

I could hardly believe my ears! She didn't feel my head or ask me a million questions like she usually did. It was as if she knew I was going to be sick. But by this time, my stomach hurt so much that I didn't care. I went back up to my room and dropped down on the bed with all my clothes on.

From the corner of my eye, I could see the red light blink on on the phone on my night stand. I knew that Mom was calling Susan.

Susan Atkins was the best friend a guy could have. You could tell Susan anything and she never laughed at you. She never told anyone what you told her, either.

Susan lived a couple of houses down the block from my house. We'd been in the same class since kindergarten, and we walked to school together nearly every day.

I picked up the remote control for the TV and turned on a cartoon. I still watched cartoons sometimes, even though they're for little kids, and I'm 12.

Suddenly, the TV screen started to wink and blink at me like a big eye. I tried to close my eyes, but I couldn't. Something was making me look. I stared at the set.

A blob of yellow-green liquid oozed out of the TV. It crept down the front of the set. It crept across the floor toward my bed. I wanted to yell for Mom, but I couldn't open my mouth. I couldn't move.

The blob crawled up the side of my bed. It crept across the bed and onto my foot. I tried to shake it off, but my leg wouldn't move. It went up my leg and then on to my chest. It felt like a heavy blanket suffocating me. It's trying to kill me, I thought. I was going to die. I couldn't breathe. I still couldn't move.

The blob crept up my neck. It zipped across my cheek. Then it stopped.

2

I let my breath out slowly. I'm still alive, I thought. Tears started in my eyes and I wanted to wipe them away with my sleeve, but I still couldn't lift my arm. I felt the blob slither backwards. Down my cheek, my neck, my chest, off my leg. The minute my foot was free, I felt the blob release its hold on me. I could move again.

I jumped off the bed and ran to the door.

From the hallway, I watched the blob ooze down my bed and across the floor, leaving no trace that it had ever been there. It flowed back up the TV set and into the screen. For a second, the screen went pitch black and then the cartoon came on again.

I tiptoed back into the room and reached out to turn off the TV. I was afraid that something inside it would reach out and grab my hand. But nothing did. I turned off the power button and turned the screen to the wall. I wondered if that blob could get out if the TV was off. I pulled out the plug. Maybe I'd never watch TV again. Maybe I should put the TV in the garage, I thought.

I headed out of my room but my reflection in the bathroom mirror stopped me. What was that scratch on my cheek? Did I have it before that blob crawled all over me? No way. I'd have remembered if I'd scratched myself there.

I went into the bathroom and put a Band-Aid on the scratch. Suddenly, I realized that my stomach didn't hurt any more.

That's so strange, I thought, looking at myself in the mirror. Now both Mom and I had Band-

Aids on our faces. I hoped Mom wouldn't decide that today was the day I had to go to the supermarket with her. I didn't want my friends teasing me that my mom and I looked like twins.

I passed my sister's room. She wasn't in her crib any more. Mom must have come upstairs and gotten her while I was in my room. I wondered if she had peeked into my room and seen the blob. I thought about asking her as I started down the stairs.

I didn't get a chance to ask, though. When I was halfway down, the doorbell rang. Mom came from the kitchen, carrying my sister. "I'll get it," she said, and opened the door.

A boy about my age stood on the porch. He had red hair like I do, only his wasn't as curly as mine or nearly as red. He was wearing jeans and a T-shirt, just like me.

He looked at Mom and then at me. "Hi," he said. "My mom and I just moved into the house across the street." He pointed to the house with the grey shutters that my dad had been trying to sell for about a year. My dad's a real estate broker.

"Come right in," Mom said to him as I came the rest of the way downstairs. Mom is always friendly to our neighbors, even the ones she doesn't know. They were always showing up at our house asking to borrow a mop or a cup of sugar or something. She closed the door behind him. The hall suddenly seemed chilly and I felt myself shivering.

"You seem to be just about Matt's age," Mom said. She put her arm around my shoulder. "This is Matt," she said, pushing me forward. "Matt, meet our new neighbor."

I held out my hand. "Hi," I said.

"Hi," he said. "My name's Chris."

We shook hands. His hand felt cold and clammy. When he let go, I snuck my hand down to my jeans and wiped it. I noticed that his face was slightly green, like he was sick and he was about to puke. Another shiver ran down my body. Just looking at him gave me the creeps.

Then I heard Mom say, "You and Chris are probably in the same class." She turned to me. "Why don't you show Chris the way to get to school, Matt?"

I tried to get out of it. "It's just a couple of blocks down that way," I said, waving my arm in the general direction of school.

But Mom didn't let me get away with it.

"You're not being very neighborly," she said. She turned to Chris. "Matt'll be glad to walk to school with you."

It looked like I was stuck with Chris the Creep. So I gave in. "OK," I said. "Just as soon as I get my books and my clarinet." I went back upstairs for my things. Mom and Chris were still standing by the door when I got back. Mom handed me a late note to give to my teacher. When did she write it? And, how did she know my stomach ache was gone? She never asked me. It's like she knew before I did that I would be going to school this morning.

Something strange was definitely going on. I was sure about that, but I couldn't figure out what it was.

I took the porch steps two at a time with Chris at my side. At the corner, a car horn honked. Susan was sitting next to her mother in the front seat. I raised my clarinet case to my shoulder, trying to block Chris from Susan's view. I really didn't want her to see me walking with him.

She leaned out the window and waved. "Hi, Matt," she shouted. "I thought I was the only one going to school late. I had to wait for Mom to come home from work to pick me up with my drums."

Susan was going to play the drums in the school band. "Sorry I can't offer you a ride to school," she called. "My drums have taken over the entire back seat." She waved again as the traffic light changed from red to green. "See you in school."

I waved back. "See you later," I shouted as the car picked up speed. I took my clarinet case off my shoulder. I wondered if she had noticed Chris. I knew that even if she did, and saw how creepy-looking Chris was, she wouldn't tease me about it. Not like some of my other friends. Susan was like that. She never said anything to hurt someone else's feelings.

Chris and I walked along for another block, side by side, neither one of us saying anything. As soon as we got to school, I told myself, I'd be rid of him. But then I started feeling that I should at least say *something* to him.

"Where do you come from?" I asked finally, trying to be polite. I didn't really care, but I couldn't think of anything else to ask him.

"Far away," Chris answered.

"Far away? Like Los Angeles?" I asked.

"I don't know where Los Angeles is," he answered. "I come from a dark place."

"That's a strange name for a city," I said. Then I decided that it was probably the translation of the name of a city someplace in Europe or Asia. I tried again. "Do you have a bike?" I asked.

Chris looked at me with a strange expression on his face, like he never heard the word *bike* before. He shook his head. "No."

This was getting stranger all the time, I thought, and tried one more time. "What games do you like to play?" I asked.

"Games?"

"Sure," I said. "Like baseball or soccer."

"We don't play any games," Chris said. "There isn't much sunlight where I used to live."

That was it! I was finished trying to talk to him. I quickened my pace and walked as fast as I could. If I hadn't had my book bag on my back and my clarinet in my hand slowing me down, I would have been running. I didn't care if I wasn't being neighborly. I didn't even want to walk with Chris any more. He sure was the weirdest kid I'd ever met. I wanted to get to school as fast as I could and get rid of him.

But about two blocks from school, we turned

the corner and I saw Mike Kreiger and his pals leaning against an iron gate in front of the movie house. They were laughing and passing a comic book around.

Mike Kreiger was the biggest kid in our school. He picked on all the other kids and took our lunch money. He cornered me once in the schoolyard last year. He wouldn't let me go until I'd turned all my pockets inside out and given him all the money I had. I was really scared he was going to beat me up. I heard he beat up one kid who didn't have any money to give him.

I didn't want him to see me, especially not with a Band-Aid on my face and creepy Chris walking by my side. I had to do something—fast.

I grabbed Chris' sleeve and pulled him back around the corner. "Let me show you a great short cut to school," I said. I led him down an alley between the bake shop and the Chinese take-out. We quickly crossed the parking lot behind the supermarket and came out at the back entrance to the school.

NIGHTMARE NEIGHBORS

It's a one-story red brick building with three sides. If you were in an airplane flying over the school, it would look like the letter *C* with corners. There's a big field next to it. In the spring, kids play baseball and basketball in that field. In the fall and winter the football team uses the field. It has bleachers along one side and lots of kids and teachers come to watch games. All the kids who live here in the town of Mayfield start out in this school in kindergarten and stay here until they finish high school.

The door of the school was open and we went inside. I dropped Chris off at the admissions office and went to my class.

Wouldn't you know it—Chris got put in my class. My teacher, Ms. Glacken, introduced Chris to the class. She made him sit in the row next to me, so I could see him out of the corner of my eye. All morning long, every time I looked over my shoulder, I saw him looking at me. It was like he was watching every move I made.

When it was lunch period, I met Susan at our favorite table against the back wall of the cafeteria. It was a great place to see everything that was happening there.

"This morning was for sure the strangest one

of my life!" I said. I unwrapped my tuna sandwich. I told her about the blob on the kitchen counter, how Mom was acting so strange, and about the Band-Aids we were both wearing. When I told her about the blob that came out of my TV and attacked me, she covered her face with her hands.

"That's gruesome," she said when I finished talking. She bit into her cheese sandwich. "Tell me about Chris."

"He came to my house right after that blob finished attacking me," I said. "Doesn't it seem strange to you that his hair's red like mine and we're the same age?"

Susan nodded. "Very strange and really creepy," she said.

In the afternoon, Ms. Glacken sent the kids trying out for the school band to the music room. Susan and I walked down the hallway. I didn't say anything. I was playing *Sunset Dreams* in my head one last time. Susan was quiet, too, but her hand beat time in the air. I knew she was practicing her song, just as I was.

When we got to the music room, Susan went to set up her drums. I took a seat in front of the room and put my clarinet on my lap. Chris walked in right behind us, carrying a violin. Where did he get that, I wondered. I thought back to when we walked to school. He wasn't carrying a violin. He wasn't carrying anything. Where had that violin come from?

Then I remembered that Chris hadn't shown up in the cafeteria for lunch period. Maybe that was when he went and borrowed the violin from the music teacher, Mr. Raymond. But then when and where did he eat lunch?

Mr. Raymond let the kids who wanted to try out for the string section go first. When it was his turn, Chris walked up to the front of the room with his violin. He ran the bow across the strings.

After hearing a few bars, Mr. Raymond walked to the front of the room. "That's enough, Chris," he said. "You play beautifully. We'd love to have you in the band."

When it was my turn, I stood up. My hands shook a little as I put the clarinet to my lips. I wasn't supposed to be nervous. I was in the band last year and I didn't get nervous, so why was this happening to me now? It must have something to do with that creepy Chris, I decided. Maybe he didn't want me to be in the band, so he put some kind of a spell on me.

That couldn't happen, I told myself. No one can put a spell on another person. It was just my imagination. Then I remembered the blob that had crept out of my TV. Was that my imagination, too? Or were these strange things really happening to me?

Because I was nervous, I made a mistake and played a wrong note, but I still got into the band. So did Susan.

When the tryout was over and all the band members selected, Mr. Raymond told us we'd be giving our first concert at the senior citizen center in three weeks. He passed around copies of the sheet music for the songs we were going to play. "I want you to practice the songs over and over again until you can play each one without making any mistakes. The first rehearsal will be after school on Thursday. So go home now and start practicing."

Susan left her drums at school; I took my clarinet home with me. We walked home together. Of course, the main topic of conversation was still Creepy Chris.

"He seems nice, a little shy, but nice. But he looks sick," Susan said. "Is he sick?"

"I don't know. He didn't say anything about

being sick," I said. "They wouldn't let him go to school if he's sick. But he *is* weird. Don't ever try to shake hands with him."

"Why not?" Susan asked.

"I made the mistake of shaking his hand when he came to my house," I told her. "His hand was so cold and clammy, I felt like I was shaking hands with an icicle." Then, as if that wasn't enough to convince her that Chris was weird, I told her about where Chris said he came from and that he didn't have a bike.

"Maybe he's poor," Susan said. "Maybe his parents can't afford to buy him a bike."

I had never thought of it like that. I ran that new idea through my mind for a minute, then remembered some of the other weird things Chris had said. "He said he doesn't play games," I told Susan. "He said there wasn't any sunlight where he comes from."

"Maybe we'd better teach him some games," said Susan as she stopped in front of her house. She unlatched the front gate and waved. "See you tomorrow."

"Bye," I said and kept walking. I didn't want to teach Chris anything. I didn't even want to see him ever again.

By the time I got to my house, Dad was home from work. He was playing with my sister on the living room floor. I told him what had happened in school and about Chris. I told him how spooky I felt when I was around Chris.

"Well, he and his mother are certainly different looking," Dad said. "But there are all kinds of people in this world. And we have to get to know them and accept them just as they are."

That's easy for him to say, I thought. Dad didn't have to walk to school with Chris or sit in the same class with him.

While we ate our dinner, Dad told Mom and me about the house he had sold to Chris's family. "Just Chris and his mother are here right now," he said. "They're waiting for the father and some other family members to arrive. Seems they have a rather large family. They're certainly the most unusual family I've ever sold a house to. All they brought with them was one piece of furniture—a TV set."

"Maybe Chris's dad is bringing the rest of the furniture," I said, although I wondered where Chris was sleeping until his dad came.

Dad turned to Mom. "You know that old black and white TV I keep in the office? The one my parents gave us when we first got married? Well, it finally broke down this afternoon. It's finished."

"Well," said Mom. "It's not surprising. We certainly got a lot of use out of that little TV. Why don't I meet you after work on Saturday? We can take a ride to the mall and see if we can get a new TV for you. And a new blender for me."

Dad laughed. "It's a date," he said.

I wanted to tell Dad he could take the one from my room. I didn't think I was ever going to look at it again. But I decided not to say anything. Maybe I'd change my mind in a couple of weeks, when I forgot about the blob oozing out of the TV. Besides, Mom and Dad sounded so happy about going to the mall together. My fingers went to my cheek. Dad noticed the Band- Aid.

"Do you and Mom belong to some sort of club whose members have to wear Band-Aids on their faces?" he asked me.

I knew he was just joking. "Very funny," I said. But I couldn't tell him how I got it. He wouldn't believe me. Anyway, I wasn't sure yet that the blob had anything to do with it.

I still had the Band-Aid on my face the next morning. Susan called just as I got out of the shower.

"I'm not going to school today," she said. "Call me tonight and let me know what I missed."

"OK, sure," I said and hung up. I got ready for school, gulped down my breakfast, and was out of the house extra early. I wanted to make sure I wouldn't run into Creepy Chris on my way to school.

I wasn't five feet from the front door when I heard someone calling, "Hey, Matt!" I turned around. It was Chris. Yuck! I was stuck with walking to school with him again. I thought of how great it would be if the Band-Aid on my cheek covered my whole face instead.

We headed down the block. Chris started talking about how great our class was and how much he liked going out in the school yard for recess. All the time, I was searching the block to make sure we wouldn't meet any of my friends.

Or Mike Kreiger and his friends.

4

I didn't get *that* lucky. As we crossed Main Street, who did we see coming around the corner and heading straight for us? Mike Kreiger and his two stupid buddies! Quickly I looked around for an escape route, but there wasn't one.

I can turn around and run, I thought. But I've seen Mike chasing kids down the block. He's fast. And I'm not. I looked at Chris. From the looks of him, I didn't think he had enough strength to run at all. Our only choice was to walk past Mike, I decided, and from the look on Mike's face, I could tell there was going to be trouble.

"There's going to be a hassle," I whispered to Chris. "Let me do all the talking." Maybe we could escape by just giving Mike our money.

I stuck my hand into the pocket of my jeans. Good thing I have my lunch money, I thought. I didn't exactly like the idea of sitting in class all afternoon with my stomach growling at me, but it was better than sitting there with a bloody lip or a black eye.

"Aren't those the same boys we saw yesterday?" Chris asked.

How did he know that? I wondered. We hadn't gotten close enough to them for Chris to see their faces. And I never said anything. "How..." I started to ask Chris.

But he stopped me. "Don't worry," he said. "They won't hurt us."

Mike and his pals marched right up to us, Mike leading the way. They stopped two feet away, hands on hips. "Well, look who's here," Mike said. "Two runts. Which one of you is gonna hand over the money first?"

He looked from me to Chris and then back again to me. Then he turned to his friends and laughed. They laughed, too.

From the corner of my eye, I saw Chris take his hand out of his pocket. He made a fist and extended his arm toward Mike. He opened his hand and, *whoosh*, a yellow-green blob flew out and glommed onto Mike's face. It looked exactly like the blob I saw on the kitchen counter yesterday. Where did Chris get *that* from?

"Ugh!" Mike cried. He covered his face with his hands, trying to pull off the blob. His pals took one look at him and ran off in opposite directions. He struggled with the blob and finally got it off his face. He threw it on the ground, turned, and ran down Main Street.

"He'll never bother us again," Chris told me. He bent and picked up the blob and put it into his pocket. "Let's go," he said.

I didn't believe what he said about Mike. I

thought instead that Mike was really going to have it in for us now. Maybe I could talk Mom and Dad into letting me transfer to another school—in another town!

I followed Chris down the block. All the time I walked, I was thinking about how to explain what Chris did when my friends asked me what had happened. News gets around pretty fast in my school. Mike was sure to tell everyone that Chris threw some gook at him. Of course, he'd say that he beat Chris up for doing it.

"Do you mind if we stop in and see your father in his office?" Chris asked suddenly.

Startled, I looked around. We were in front of my dad's office. Why would Chris want to visit Dad at his office?

5

"My mom wants me to find out something about our new house," Chris said as we stood in front of Dad's real estate office.

"Can't she call him on the phone?" I asked. "We'll be late for school."

"We don't have a telephone yet," Chris said. "Please, Matt. It'll just take a minute. It's very important."

"Sure, OK," I said. We went inside.

Dad's secretary told us to go right in. Dad was sitting behind his desk. He put down the papers he was looking at. "What can I do for you boys?" he asked.

"Chris's mother wants to know something," I said and dropped into the big chair in front of the desk.

Chris stood next to me. He lifted his arm and pointed his finger at Dad. His finger got longer and longer. It flowed across Dad's desk, up his arm, up his shoulder, and onto his neck. I couldn't move. I just kept staring straight ahead. Dad didn't move either. I saw the yellow-green finger zip across Dad's chin and stop. Then it started moving backwards from where it came. There was a small spot of blood on Dad's chin.

I blinked and glanced sideways at Chris. His finger had returned to normal. He was smiling at Dad. "Thanks, Mr. Beaman," he said, as if nothing unusual had happened. "My mom will sure appreciate what you've done for her."

Dad looked kind of confused. He shook his

head like he was trying to clear his mind. "Sure, no problem," he mumbled and turned to pick up the phone. Then he looked at the phone in his hand like he didn't know why it was there, and hung it up again.

"I forgot something at home," Chris said to me. "I'll see you in school." He turned and hurried out of Dad's office.

"Did you see what happened?" I asked Dad, who still looked kind of dazed and confused.

"What happened?" Dad asked.

"Chris's finger got longer and longer," I said. "It crept across your desk and up to your chin."

"That's impossible," Dad said. "People's fingers don't grow like that." His hand went to his chin. He looked at the drop of blood on his finger. "I must have nicked myself while I was shaving."

"You shaved this morning, Dad. It was hours ago," I reminded him. "The blood would be dry by now. Besides, I *saw* Chris do it." I jumped up from the chair.

"It was just your imagination," Dad said. The phone rang and he turned to answer it.

That was when I realized that Dad didn't remember what had happened. Chris must have put him in some kind of trance. I decided not to wait around and try to convince Dad that I was right. He'd never believe me, just as I never would have believed it myself yesterday. I turned and left, shaking my head.

In school, all I could think of was what Chris had done. Questions kept jumping around in my mind. Why did he deliberately scratch Dad's face? And why did Mom and I both have scratches on our faces? What were those blobs? Where did my nightmare neighbors come from and why were they here? Who *was* Chris?

In band practice, I couldn't concentrate on playing. I was so bad that Mr. Raymond told me to go home. I took my book bag out of my locker, shut the door, and put the lock on it.

As I walked toward the front entrance, I saw Mike Kreiger come out of the principal's office. I stopped dead in my tracks. After what happened between him and Chris this morning, I was sure he was going to do something terrible to me. Just because I was there. Besides, he probably thought Chris was my friend.

But all Mike did was look at me, turn, and hurry away. There was a strange look on his face. It was almost like he was *afraid* of me.

I couldn't believe it! Chris was right. Mike *wasn't* going to bother either one of us any more.

As I walked home, I thought about Chris and his long finger creeping across Dad's desk. It looked like the same kind of stuff that crept out of my TV, the same as the blob on the kitchen counter, and like the stuff Chris threw at Mike Kreiger. Somehow, they were all connected. But I still couldn't figure out what they were and what they were doing here in Mayfield.

That's why I started wishing Susan were with me. I could always talk to her about things that were bothering me. Even though she also was only 12, she could figure out important things better than anyone else I knew. Mom said Susan was mature for her age.

But Susan was still at home sick, so I had to think things out for myself. I thought that maybe there might be some clues in Chris's house. I decided to look into one of their windows and see if I could find out anything there.

At my corner, I veered to the left and crossed the street. I stood in front of Chris's house for a minute. No one seemed to be home. I started up the empty driveway and quietly crept around to the back of the house.

The windows on the first floor were very high up. I stood on tiptoes and tried to see inside, but I wasn't tall enough. I looked around the back yard and found an old crate leaning up against the fence. It felt strong enough to hold my weight, so I stood it against the house and climbed onto it. The windows had blinds on them and they were closed, but not all the way. I could see inside.

I saw an empty kitchen. I mean really *empty!* There was nothing in the room—no table, no refrigerator, nothing.

Then I heard footsteps behind me.

I whirled around and looked into the face of a woman about the same height as my mother. Her hair was blond like my mother's. But her skin was the same sickly-looking color as Chris's.

"Oh, I'm sorry," I stammered.

The woman didn't seem to notice that anything was wrong. She smiled pleasantly. "You must be looking for Chris," she said. "He's in his room. Come inside and you two can have some milk and cookies."

I didn't want to go inside. All I wanted to do was *look* inside. Suddenly, I didn't feel safe. I felt as if something terrible was going to happen to me. I wanted to turn and run down the driveway toward my own house. But I couldn't. Someone— or something—was making me follow Chris's mother. She led me around to the front of the house and up the steps.

The door opened and I followed her inside. We stood in the living room and she called Chris to come downstairs. "You can wait for him in the living room. There are milk and cookies for you in there," she told me. Then she disappeared into the kitchen behind the stairs.

I wondered where she got the milk from. There was no refrigerator in the kitchen. I walked into the living room and put my clarinet and book bag down on the floor near the open entrance way. I looked around. Dad was right. The only thing in there was a TV set. And on it was a tray with moldy-green cookies and two glasses of milk that looked as if they had some pistachio syrup stirred into them. I was getting really scared. How did she know I was coming?

All the shades were drawn and the room was dark. I shivered. It was very cool. There was a musty smell in the living room, like no one had opened a window in the whole year since someone had lived in the house. How could anyone live in a place like this? Then I remembered that Chris was used to living in a dark place. But I felt like I was in some sort of spooky cave. I looked around, expecting to find a monster in the corner, or a ghost waiting to grab me and kill me. I had to get out of there before something really bad happened to me.

Just as I reached for my things on the floor, Chris came down the stairs, blocking my escape route to the front door. "Hi, Matt," he said.

"Oh . . . hi," I said. "Your mother invited me in."

"I'm glad you came," he said. "I've never had a friend come to visit me."

I thought about telling him that I wasn't his friend and that I was only there because his mom made me come in. But I decided I'd better not. If he could put a spell on Dad and make Mike Kreiger afraid of me, there was no telling what he would do if he got mad at me. He might even try to kill me with a blob of that gunk he kept in his pocket.

But I *had* to get out of there. I took a sideways step out of the room.

"Who have we got here?" A man's booming voice came from inside the living room. I spun around. A man stood in front of the TV. He reminded me a little of Dad, except that his skin was the same shade of yellow-green as Chris's and his mother's.

Where had he come from? Had he been hiding in the darkness of the living room when I first came in? Or did he just come out of the TV?

Chris didn't appear to be the least bit surprised. "Hi, Dad. This is my friend, Matt," he said. "He's in my class at school."

Chris's father came closer. He held out his hand to me. Reluctantly, I held out mine and shook hands with him. His hand felt as cold and clammy as Chris's had.

"Dad just got here today," Chris said.

"And happy I am to be here, I can tell you that," said his father.

Chris's mother came back to join us in the living room. She pointed to the tray on top of the TV. "Help yourselves to some milk and cookies," she said.

Chris reached for a cookie and a glass of milk. He stuffed the cookie into his mouth and gobbled it down. He downed half of the milk in one big long gulp. "Wow! I love this stuff," he said, wiping his mouth with his hand. He looked at me. "Aren't you having any?" he asked.

I remembered the greenish eggs Mom had cooked that gave me that stomach ache. I groaned inside, wondering if the milk and cookies would have the same effect on me. I didn't want to go through that again. I shook my head and thought fast. "Can't," I said. "We're having dinner early tonight. Mom will kill me if I don't have an appetite."

"We're so anxious for our daughter to get here," said Chris's mother.

"When is she coming?" I asked, glad to get their attention off my not having any of their milk and cookies.

"We're not really sure," said Chris's father.

"Is she older or younger than Chris?" I asked, thinking how proud Mom would be of me for being so neighborly. But all the while, I was trying to think of a way to end the conversation and get out of the house.

"Older," said Chris's mother.

"Younger," said Chris's father at the same time.

"She's a baby," said Chris.

That's when I saw a way out. "I really have to go home and take care of *my* baby sister," I said. For a second, I thought that maybe they wouldn't let me leave. But no one made a move to stop me. I picked up my book bag and clarinet off the floor.

Chris walked me to the front door. "See you in school," he said.

"Come again soon," Chris's parents called from behind him as I went out onto the porch.

I crossed the street to my house and went up to my room. Funny how Chris's parents didn't know how old their own daughter was. They were just as strange as Chris was! I wondered if his sister would turn out to be as creepy as the rest of her family. From my window, I saw Mom pushing Amy in the backyard swing.

I looked at my baby sister. Somehow, I knew she was the clue to Chris's sister.

They had gotten blood from Mom, from Dad, and from me. Now they had a mother, a father, and a son my own age with red hair like mine.

Would they do something to Amy so they could get their daughter into their house?

7

I called Susan. "You didn't miss much at school," I said. "Ms. Glacken was absent and the substitute said we could do whatever we wanted so long as we were quiet and sat in our seats."

"What happened in science?" Susan asked. Science was her best subject. "Did we get to fill in the parts on that frog diagram?"

"We started to when the bell rang," I said. "Mr. Bedloe told us to finish it for homework."

"Good," Susan said. "I have my diagram here. I'll do it tonight What else?"

"That's it for what happened in class. I really messed up in band practice, though, and Mr. Raymond told me to go home before practice ended," I said. "On the way, I went over to Chris's house. I wasn't going to go in, just look around from outside. Well, his mom caught me peeking in the kitchen window and made me go inside. She wanted me to eat these yucky cookies she had. Chris ate them, but I didn't."

"Ohhhh!" said Susan. "I wish I'd been there."

"I wish you had, too," I said. "Then there was this weird conversation. You should have heard them—Chris's mom and his dad and Chris, too. They started talking about Chris's sister. They said she was coming here."

"What was weird about that?"

"Well, Chris's mom said she's older than Chris. His dad said she's younger. And Chris said she was a baby," I told her. "Doesn't it seem weird to you that they don't know how old she is?"

Susan agreed. "Really weird," she said.

"I think they're going to do something to Amy so they can bring Chris's sister here," I said.

"What makes you think that?"

"Well," I said. "First, Mom got that scratch on her forehead. Then, that blob came out of the TV and attacked me. Right after that, Chris and his mom bought their house from my dad."

"So?"

"Then, Chris's finger scraped my dad's chin and right after that his dad was in their house," I said. "Now, they're saying Chris's sister is coming. And Chris knows I have a baby sister. He saw Mom holding her on the morning he came to my house to introduce himself. So it just seems to me that they're going to do something weird to Amy too."

Susan and I talked for a couple more minutes, trying to figure out what would happen. But neither of us could figure it out.

I kept thinking about it after we hung up and for the rest of the afternoon. No good idea came to me. After dinner, when I went back up to my room, I thought about it again. I was supposed to finish my frog diagram and practice the clarinet, but I couldn't concentrate on either one. All I could think about was what horrible thing Chris and his family might do to my baby sister. Thinking so hard for so long made me tired, and I got into bed.

Before I knew it, it was morning and I was still no closer to an answer than I'd been the night before. I just wanted to keep my eyes open, and since it was Saturday, I was able to stick close to my sister. She was in her highchair in the kitchen when I came down for breakfast, chewing on a piece of bagel. "Ahhh!" she said when she saw me.

I went over to her and rubbed the top of her head. "Good morning, princess," I said. I sat down at the table next to Dad.

Dad put down his newspaper and smiled at me. " 'Morning, fellow," he said. "Got anything good planned for today?"

I knew he wouldn't understand if I told him I was just going to make sure that nothing bad happened to my sister. "Not really," I said instead. "I'm just going to hang around here."

"Didn't you make any plans with your friend Chris?" Dad asked, taking a sip of coffee.

I shook my head. "Chris isn't my friend, and I don't plan on doing *anything* with him *ever!*"

"But he saved you from those boys yesterday," Mom said, bringing a glass of orange juice to the table. She set it in front of me. "His mother told me," she added quickly.

Bet she didn't tell you *how* he did it, I thought. I looked at Mom. She still had that strange look on her face. Maybe she did know, like she knew my stomach ache went away.

"I'm just going to hang around the house," I said again. I took a swallow of orange juice.

Dad took another sip of coffee and pushed himself back from the table. "Got to get started selling those houses," he said. Dad always worked on Saturday and Sunday. Those were the days people usually went looking for houses.

"I'll walk you to the door," Mom said. "Don't forget we're going shopping at the mall afterwards." She turned back to me. "Matt, be a pal and watch Amy till I come back."

"Sure, OK," I said. I put down the juice and walked over to my sister. I covered my face with my hands. "Peek-a-boo!" I said, uncovering my face. My sister giggled. It was her favorite game.

I looked at the TV on the counter. It was on again without the sound. Then I saw a yellow-green blob on the counter in front of it. I knew it wasn't the one from the other day. That one was gone by the time I'd come home from school.

I covered my face with my hands again and did another peek-a-boo for my sister. When I took my hands away, the blob wasn't in the same place.

It had moved.

I looked again. Right in front of me, it moved forward, putting out tentacles like an octopus. It crept down the side of the counter and onto the floor. It was heading straight for the highchair!

Suddenly, I knew how Chris's sister was getting here. Somehow, this blob was going to bring her. The same way other blobs had brought Chris and his parents. More than likely, Chris or his parents had sent this blob to my house. And it had gotten here through the TV on the

112

counter! And it was coming for my sister!

I remembered again how scared I'd been when the blob had made its way out of my TV and crept up my body. I didn't want that to happen to my sister. She was too little to have such a thing happen to her. She'd be scared for the rest of her life. I had to stop this blob before it got to her!

I wanted to hit it with Mom's apron. But I couldn't lift my arm to pick it up. I tried to scream for Mom, but I couldn't open my mouth. I stared at the blob as it slithered across the kitchen floor, closer and closer to Amy.

I concentrated all my strength in my right foot and willed it to move. Move! Move! Move! I shouted in my head. I looked down at my foot and then looked to where I wanted it to go. Suddenly, my foot moved.

The hold the blob had on me was gone. I grabbed Mom's apron from the counter and swiped it at the blob. But it just kept on oozing slowly across the floor. My sister thought I was playing a new game and she giggled. She liked this new game just as much as the peek-a-boo one. She had no idea of the danger she was in at that very moment.

The blob kept putting out its yellow-green tentacles and creeping closer and closer to the highchair. The apron was useless. I threw it back on the counter and stamped on the blob with my foot. My shoe made a squishing sound as it made contact. The blob oozed out around my shoe and kept right on moving.

The squishing sound was the same one my shoes made whenever I walked home from school in the rain and they got soaked. That's when I realized that the blob was made of water.

"That's it!" I shouted into the air. I knew how to stop it!

My shout startled my sister and she started to cry. But I didn't have time now to make her stop crying.

I raced out of the kitchen and up the stairs to the bathroom. I unplugged the blow dryer and hurried back downstairs with it. I plugged it into the electrical outlet next to the TV and turned it to the hottest setting. I aimed the hot air right at the blob.

The blob stopped moving. It jiggled back and forth for a second, as if it were trying to get away from the hot air. Then, slowly, it shriveled and shriveled until there was only a greenish stain on the kitchen floor.

I shoved the blow dryer into the waist of my jeans, scooped up the electric cord, and tucked it into my pocket. "Need to get rid of any more blobs?" I asked my sister. "Just call Matt, the Blob Killer." My sister stopped crying and giggled, reaching out her arms to me. Then she gnawed at the piece of bagel again.

If only I'd thought of the blow dryer when that blob oozed its way out of my TV and crawled all over me. I could have gotten rid of it the same way. Then I thought that maybe Chris and his parents might send another blob! There was just one thing to do to make sure they never did. I couldn't stay home forever to watch my sister.

Mom came back from walking Dad to the car. She looked at me, at my sister, and then at the stain on the kitchen floor. She still seemed sort of dazed, as if she had woken up in the middle of the night and didn't know exactly where she was. Kind of how Dad acted in his office after Chris had made his finger return to normal.

"What happened?" she asked in a strange voice.

"I'll explain later," I said, and I rushed past her. "I've got to call Susan." I had to make *this* call from my room. I didn't want my mom to hear me. She'd never believe me. I didn't blame her. I wouldn't either, if someone told me that a blob of watery stuff could move or that someone's finger could get longer. Those things only happened in stories, I thought, like Pinocchio's nose that got longer whenever he told a lie. I took the stairs two at a time. I put the blow dryer back in the bathroom on my way.

I got lucky. Susan was home. "I'm helping my mom vacuum," she said. "I'll be finished in about an hour."

I couldn't wait that long. "I have to talk to you *now*," I said. "It can't wait. You have to come over right away."

"I'll ask my mom," Susan said. "Hold on a minute." Then she came back on the phone. "My mom says I can come over as soon as I finish the living room. Are you OK?"

"No," I said. "Something very strange is going on. I'll tell you all about it when you get here. Hurry!"

Susan was at my house in ten minutes. I

waited for her on the porch. "What happened?" she asked as she sat down on the top step.

"Someone in Chris's family sent a blob to my house through the kitchen TV," I said. "It tried to attack my sister. That's how they're trying to bring Chris's sister to Mayfield from wherever they come from."

"Oh, my goodness," said Susan, pressing her palms flat against her cheeks. "Did it hurt her?"

"It never touched her," I said. "It was made of water. I zapped it with a blow dryer."

"Do you think they'll try again?"

"That's exactly what I'm afraid of," I said. There's got to be a way to stop them from trying again. If I went over to Chris's house again, maybe I could find a way to make them stop doing it."

"Would you *really* go back there again?" Susan asked.

"I'm really scared. But I'm more scared that they'll attack my sister again. Next time they might really hurt her or kill her."

"They won't kill her," she said. "People in Mayfield don't kill other people."

"They're not real people!" I said. "Real people don't have yellow-green skin. They don't have watery hands. Maybe they're made of the same stuff the blobs are made of."

Susan became very quiet. She leaned her elbow on her knee and rested her chin on her hand. She was thinking. Then she stood up. "We can go together," she said. "They won't try to kill both of us."

We found Chris and his parents sitting on the grass in their back yard. They had their faces tilted up to the sun. I felt a little safer being outside. I didn't think they'd try anything long as they didn't drag us into the house.

I tried acting very cool. "Is your sister here yet?" I asked Chris.

Chris shook his head. "Oh, no," he said. "She can't come just yet."

I felt helpless. I didn't know what else to say to them.

"See, what did I tell you?" I asked Susan when we were on our way back across the street. "That proves that they tried to get Chris's sister here through Amy. When I zapped that blob, they gave up on his sister."

I was relieved that my sister was safe. But somehow I knew that I still wasn't finished with Chris and his crazy family. I was right.

Two weeks later, Susan and I were walking home together after band practice. It was the last rehearsal before our concert at the senior citizen center. From behind us, we heard Chris's voice calling, "Oh, Matt! Oh, Susan!" We stopped, turned around, and waited until Chris, carrying his violin, caught up to us.

"Good news," Chris said. "My grandparents are coming."

"Will they be here in time for the concert tomorrow?" Susan asked.

"Oh, no," said Chris. "They can't come until *after* the concert."

We walked, not talking. I was thinking about what Chris had said. His grandparents couldn't come until after the concert. Not *wouldn't*, but *couldn't*. I remembered that his dad didn't come until after our visit to Dad's office. Chris didn't show up until after the blob came at me from out of the TV. And Chris's sister never came because I didn't let that blob get to Amy.

On the night of the concert, Susan and I went to the senior citizen center together. "We're going to have to watch Chris during the concert," I said as we approached the building.

"That's not going to be easy," Susan said.

"We're also going to have to watch Mr. Raymond's baton."

"I know," I said. "But I know that something is definitely going to happen at the concert. Something very bad."

9

The senior citizen center is on Main Street next to the library. It's in a low stone building with a wheelchair ramp in front, so people who can't walk can get in. Once, while Susan and I went skating, the gate in the fence was open. We had a great time speed-skating down that ramp until the custodian came out and told us not to do it any more.

I waited outside the gate with Susan until the school bus pulled up and Mr. Raymond unloaded her drums. It took us a couple of trips up the winding path to get all of the drums inside. Other band members came, too, bringing their instruments.

We set up our chairs in a semicircle in the music room. There was a piano in one corner and room for Susan to set up her drums in the other.

Then we made rows of chairs for the audience. As soon as we sat down and began to tune our instruments, the room started to fill up.

I looked out at the audience. There were dozens of grandmothers and grandfathers.

Suddenly, I knew why Chris said his grandparents couldn't come until *after* the concert. I remembered how his finger had begun to grow in Dad's office. He was going to do the same thing right here! I turned and looked at Chris sitting with the string section. He was too far away to touch anyone, so he probably couldn't do anything right out in the open. Besides, I didn't think he could put his spell on so many people at one time.

When everyone was seated and ready for the concert to begin, a tall woman got up and came to the front of the room. She stood facing us. She said she was the director of the center. "We'd like to welcome you and thank you for coming," she said. "During the intermission, our members would be pleased to give you a complete tour of our center."

As soon as she said that, I knew when Chris would make his move. When the seniors were showing us around. That's when he could get close enough to them. I didn't know how I was going to stop him, but I knew I had to.

Mr. Raymond took his place in front of us. He raised his baton and the concert began.

I couldn't concentrate on the music. I had to think of a plan to stop Chris. There wouldn't be much time during the intermission. I pretended to be playing my clarinet, the way a singer sometimes lip-synchs to a record, and kept trying to think of what to do. Only Mr. Raymond would know that I wasn't really playing. I would think of an explanation for him later. Besides, it was better to pretend-play than to play wrong notes and ruin the concert for everyone.

The first part of the concert ended. I still had no plan. We stood up and bowed as the seniors clapped their hands. We sat down again. The seniors just kept right on clapping. Mr. Raymond motioned to us to stand up again and take another bow. When we finally sat down again, I motioned to Susan that I needed to talk to her. When the clapping finally stopped, she pushed her way through the crowd.

"What's up?" she whispered when she joined me.

"Just stick close to me," I whispered back.

"He's going to do it during the intermission."

The members of the center surrounded us and split us into groups of two and three. A tiny woman with a white braid twisted around the top of her head was our guide. "Hello," she said. "My name is Mrs. Ethel Ettington and it's my pleasure to show you around. Follow me, please." She turned and started for the door of the music room. Susan and I followed. I stopped and grabbed Chris and told him to follow her with us. At least I could keep an eye on him and keep him with us.

We walked out of the music room and down a brightly lit hallway. The walls were decorated with framed paintings and photographs. "These were done by our members," said Mrs. Ettington. "Some of them are very good and have won awards."

She led us past a closed door with the words *Beauty Salon* on it. Mrs. Ettinger pushed it open. We looked inside. There were mirrors on two of the walls and a couple of barber chairs. The smell of hair spray was so sicky-sweet it nearly made me puke. But Mrs. Ettinger didn't seem to notice. "Here's where we come to make ourselves beautiful," she smiled. "Some of our members were hairdressers in their younger days."

Mrs. Ettinger continued on down the hall and took us next into a large kitchen. "We do our own cooking and baking here," she said, stopping in front of the stove. "Many of us prefer to come to the center to eat our meals, especially those of us who live alone. It's nice to have a friend to talk to when we have our meals."

I could still smell the faint odor of food in the kitchen. The seniors had definitely had apple pie for dessert.

Then, out of the corner of my eye, I saw Chris's arm move. He was going to do it right here, I thought! Right in front of Susan and me. I watched his arm come up. His finger extended toward Mrs. Ettinger. I saw her eyes get wide with fear. I willed my head to turn toward Susan. She didn't move. She just stared at Chris's moving finger.

I had to do something fast. Mrs. Ettinger was an old woman. She could have a heart attack and die if she were scared. I just couldn't let that happen. I focused my attention on my feet. Move! Move! Move! I shouted at them inside my head. It had worked for me before—in the kitchen when the blob was going after my sister.

My right foot moved forward. My left foot followed. I was free. I saw that Susan was still just standing there, gaping at the scene in front of her. She was under Chris's spell and of no use in saving Mrs. Ettinger. It was all up to me.

The beauty salon flashed into my mind. That's where I would find what I needed to save Mrs. Ettinger. I raced out of the kitchen and back down the hall. The door of the beauty salon was still open so I dashed inside. There on the counter was the tool I was looking for—a blow dryer! I grabbed it and raced back to the kitchen.

Chris's finger was slowly making its way up Mrs. Ettinger's leg when I got there. I searched the kitchen wall for the closest electrical outlet. I found it, and plugged the blow dryer in and turned it on full blast.

"Matt, what are you doing?" Chris cried. His finger shrivelled up until it became as thin as the reed in my clarinet. "All I need is just a bit of her skin. She won't be hurt, and it'll mean so much to my grandparents!"

Now I knew for sure what the blob wanted

from my sister, and why Mom and Dad and I all had scratches on our faces. The blobs had taken pieces of our skin! I shuddered. Chris and his family weren't real people. They were made of a watery substance and used our skin, the skin of real people, as a disguise. For a second I wondered where that dark place far away was that Chris said he came from. Surely it wasn't any place on this earth.

I aimed the nozzle of the blow dryer at Chris. "No, Matt. Please! Don't!" he screamed.

But I had to. I turned on the heat and watched Chris shrivel up and disappear. When all that was left of him was a round stain on the floor, I turned off the dryer.

At about the same time, Susan and Mrs. Ettinger shook their heads and looked around.

"Oh, dear," Mrs. Ettinger said. "Did I forget something?"

"What happened?" Susan asked.

"I'll tell you later," I whispered. "When we're alone."

"What happened to that nice young man who was with us?" Mrs. Ettinger asked.

"He had to leave," I said. "He was in a hurry to go."

"He's really gone," I whispered to Susan as we turned back the way we'd come.

No one seemed to notice that Chris wasn't with us during the rest of the concert. Afterwards, Susan and I walked home together. I told her what had happened in the kitchen and how Chris had disappeared when I turned the blow dryer on him.

"There's just one more thing to do," I said. "I've got to get rid of Chris's parents."

We looked at each other.

10

"I've got to do it," I told Susan. "Otherwise, they'll just keep coming and coming after more people. Sooner or later, someone's going to get hurt or even die."

"You can't just go up to them and zap them with the blow dryer," Susan said. "You can't just do that to people."

"But I did it to Chris," I said. "Besides, they're not really people. They're just globs of water dressed up to look like people. You have to remember that."

"OK. Then let me go with you," she said. "I have a blow dryer. If we use two of them, we can zap them both at the same time. This way, one can't get away or try to hurt us."

That was fine with me. I didn't really want to go back to Chris's house by myself.

We went to my house first. Mom and Dad were watching TV in the living room. They looked up as we came in.

"How was the concert?" Mom asked.

"Great!" I said. I looked at Susan. "Why don't you tell them about the concert while I go upstairs for a minute?"

"OK," Susan said, sitting down on the sofa next to Mom. "The senior citizens really were happy that we came."

I took the stairs two at a time and grabbed the blow dryer out of the bathroom. I tucked it into my waist and stuck the cord into my pocket. Matt the Blob Killer was ready to go!

Susan stood up as I came back to the living room. "I'm going over to Susan's for a while," I told Mom and Dad.

"Don't be late," Dad said. Mom waved goodbye and turned back to the TV.

"Sure, OK," I said. I hurried Susan out of the house. We raced each other down the block to Susan's house. Susan won; she didn't have the blow dryer to slow her down.

There was a note taped to the refrigerator in Susan's house. "Hi, honey," it said in the red ink her mother liked to use. "I've gone to the movies with my friend Janine."

That saved us the trouble of having to explain where we were going. We doubled back and crossed the street to Chris's house. This time, we headed straight for the front door and knocked.

Chris's mother opened the door. "Chris isn't home from the concert yet," she said. "But come right in anyway." She led the way into the living room, which still had only the TV set in it. Chris's father stood in front of the TV.

"Nice to see you both again," he said. Then he looked down at the blow dryer, which was sticking out of my jeans. "What's that you've got there?"

I looked down. Was it possible that he didn't know what it was? I pulled it out and pointed it at him. This was going to be easier than I thought. "It's called a blow dryer," I said. "It makes blasts of hot air come out and dries your hair in no time at all."

"Or your nails when you polish them," Susan quickly added.

"Let me show you how it works," I said, looking around for an electrical outlet. They all followed me to the corner of the room. I bent and plugged the blow dryer into the outlet near the floor. Susan bent and plugged hers in too.

"Ready?" I asked Susan. She nodded. "At the count of three, we turn them on. One . . . two . . . three!" Both of us pushed the buttons and two blasts of hot air shot out of the nozzles. They hit their targets at the same time.

As Chris's mother began to shrink, she called out, "Please, don't do that. We didn't mean to harm anyone."

"We just wanted to feel the sunshine's warmth," said Chris's father, who was now about half his original size. "It's so cold and damp far down beneath the earth where we come from."

"We just took a tiny bit of human skin for each of us," Chris's mother said. "We duplicated your skin to make enough to cover us, so we wouldn't be discovered."

"How did you get here?" asked Susan.

"Through the TV," said Chris's father. "That's a direct route to where we live."

A minute later, both of them were just two yellow-green stains on the floor. Susan and I turned off the dryers and pulled the plugs out of the sockets. Then we went out of the house and closed the door. We looked at each other, not happy exactly, but relieved.

A couple of mornings later, Susan got to my house a little early. I was still sitting in the kitchen finishing breakfast. Dad was running late, so he was still drinking his coffee. Mom invited Susan to join us, and set a bowl of cereal in front of her.

Dad put down his newspaper. "You know, the strangest thing happened yesterday. I went by Chris's house. Thought I'd stop in and see how his family was doing." Dad looked straight at me. "No one was there. The house was completely empty. Even the TV was gone. It's as if they just disappeared into thin air."

Mom came to the table. "Have you seen Chris recently?" she asked.

Susan and I looked at each other and shook our heads.

It was funny how we had both already begun

to forget the whole crazy experience. Chris, with his weird yellow-green skin, his mother and father, the empty house with only a TV, it was already fading into memory.

"I guess he went back to wherever he came from," I said. "A dark, faraway place."

CAMP FEAR

by Claudia Vurnakes

1

"What the...?" I froze, my hand outstretched.

I had just reached for one of Marco's brownies from home. That's when I heard it—the tremendous explosion that started all our troubles.

We were on the beach at Sea Dune, a camp for kids that combined studying the environment with waterfront sports. We, the guys from Tent Seven, had been taking a snack break before heading for some beach fun.

Suddenly, we heard a giant crash, like thunder. But it was the middle of a bright sunny day.

Nosey, the official Camp Sea Dune mascot dog, was the first down the beach. He ran in the direction of the science lab. We shoved the leftover snacks into our backpacks and started after him. Dean and Gene were the fastest runners. They were identical twins who did everything together. Lollipop and I were close behind. Lolli was my best friend at camp. He always had some kind of candy in his mouth. So we all started calling him Lollipop. As usual, Marco was last.

He was the only weirdo in Tent Seven, a real noodle. He whined and complained about everything. The only reason we put up with him was the care packages he got from home. His mom made fabulous brownies. The best.

We followed Nosey down the wet sand as far as we could. When the sand gave way to the ocean, we scrambled up a steep bank. Here, we slowed down some. Clumps of bushes and tall sea grass made it harder to run. Nosey got so far ahead we couldn't see him anymore.

That's when Marco started coughing. Soon the rest of us noticed it, too. The air. Something strange was in the air. Tiny bits of hot stinging sand, so small you couldn't see them. But you sure could feel them. It hurt to breathe. It hurt bad! First that awful noise, and now this. Something terrible must have happened down at the science lab.

Running out in front, Dean and Gene came to a dead stop.

"Watch it, you two!" I yelled. But not quickly enough. I slammed into them from behind. Then I saw why they had stopped. It was Nosey.

Up ahead of Dean and Gene, the little dog lay sprawled out on the path. His brown fuzzy body was gray all over, from the tip of his nose to the end of his tail. It was sand. Nosey was covered with sand! He didn't move. He just panted and whimpered softly.

I looked closer. Unbelievable! He had a small green ball in his mouth. Nosey must have nabbed one of my seaweed cookies! He still had it in his mouth!

Oh yeah, I'd better explain. My mom is a health food nut. Most mothers send candy and gum and brownies to their kids at camp. I get stuff that's supposed to be good for you, like cookies made out of seaweed. Yuck-o!

I started to go over to poor Nosey, but Marco suddenly grabbed my arm.

"Look!" he gasped. A thin smoky cloud floated in the air above the little dog.

As we stared in amazement, a shadowy figure came out of nowhere. One minute there was just Nosey, panting on the ground. The next minute there was a strange man, some guy I had never seen before, leaning over him.

I gulped in disbelief. The man took Mom's seaweed cookie right out from Nosey's mouth!

The mysterious figure stood up.

He saw us staring.

He stared back.

That's when I first saw his eyes. Fiery red eyes. Scary, hypnotic eyes. They seemed to drill a hole right through my head. Red-hot daggers started stabbing my brain. Someone let out a soft, scared moan. It was me!

It took every ounce of strength I had. But I did it. I tore my eyes away. I looked away from that face with the awful red eyes.

I blinked and shook my head. I blinked again. Was I going crazy? The man looked as if he were made of gray clouds. I could even see tree limbs and bushes where his arms and legs should have been. I realized I was looking right through his body!

Who—what—was this guy?

Then, without a sound, without a movement, the man dematerialized. I guess that's what you'd call it. Suddenly, he just wasn't there. Gone. Vanished.

Only a tiny puff of gray smoke remained where, a second before, the man had been.

For what seemed like hours, no one even breathed.

The smoke drifted away toward the sea.

Then Lolli exploded. "What was that? Was it a—" His voice died out.

We stared at one another, our eyes big as frisbees. The word Lollipop couldn't say was the same word we all were thinking.

Ghost.

We had just seen a real ghost! What was a ghost doing here?

All at once, we remembered poor Nosey, lying on the ground. We rushed over. Dean and Gene bent down to pat the little fellow.

Nosey tried to lift his head, but it was too late. His eyes closed, and he gave a sad little whimper. Then he was still.

Lolli gulped. "Is he d-dead?"

Dean shook his head. "Not dead, just . . . "

Gene finished the sentence in a puzzled voice, "...sleeping!"

2

We ran back into camp, feet and hearts pounding. All five of us stopped for breath and looked around. It was suppertime, and all the campers were heading for the dining hall. It was so odd—everything seemed perfectly normal!

Guys were laughing, talking, joking around as they always did. No one mentioned the explosion down by the lab. No one looked worried. No one acted as if he had seen anything unusual, anything like a ghost.

Lolli stopped a couple of younger kids.

"Hey, what's going on with Skull and Max? They've done another crazy experiment, right? You know, the explosion?"

The two boys gave Lolli a strange look. One of them pointed to the dining hall.

"Lollipop, too much candy is bad for your brain. Skull and Max are right inside, eating supper!"

They walked off, leaving all of us scratching

our heads. It was too confusing.

Had no one else heard the explosion or seen the strange smoky figure? Were all five of us sunstroked out of our heads? Had we just imagined the whole thing?

Skull was Dr. Skelnic, our camp director. He was a famous scientist. He looked really weird because he had lost all his hair in some experiment, even his eyebrows. The kids all called him Skull behind his back. But if he caught you, watch out!

Max was Dr. Skelnic's goofy assistant. During the day, he helped in the lab. At night, he told dumb campfire stories that were supposed to scare you. Monsters, blood, guts—stuff like that.

Together, Skull and Max were trying to solve the mystery of the island. Which was seaweed. Not one speck of the slimy green stuff could be found anywhere near here. Personally, I never missed the seaweed. But Skull and Max did all kinds of strange experiments in the camp lab, trying to find out what kept seaweed from growing here.

Now, whether or not anyone else knew it, Camp Sea Dune had something much scarier than seaweed to worry about.

"Come on, guys. Let's eat. I'm hungry." That was Marco.

It figured. We had just heard a mysterious explosion and seen a ghost come out of nowhere to coma-tize a poor innocent dog, and Marco was hungry.

"You're kidding, right?" I said. "Who could eat at a time like this? I don't know about the rest of you, but I've got some serious thinking to do."

I turned for the tent. Lolli started after me. Dean and Gene nodded, like two heads fastened on one stick.

But Marco kept pleading. "Aw, come on, guys!" he whined. "It's meatloaf and spinach night. Please!"

Then he grinned his sneaky little grin. He knew he had something we couldn't refuse.

"Stay and eat, Josh, and I'll give you more brownies!!"

He had us there. We all sat down in the dining hall. But only Marco ate anything. I just pushed the food around on my plate. Dean and Gene didn't eat either. Even Lolli stopped after a couple of bites.

But not Marco. That skinny little guy ate as if he'd never seen food before. He finished his plate, then speared the meatloaf on mine. He talked, too. Nonstop.

"So, what do you think it was? Did we all see the same thing? Was it really a ghost? I have never actually believed in ghosts, but after today, well, I'm not so sure." Marco reached for my vegetables.

He felt his forehead. "I don't think I'm sick. Are you sick, Josh? We don't have sunstroke or anything like that, do we? It was a real ghost, right? What do you think brought him to life? Something must have called him up from wherever it is ghosts stay—"

He stopped. He saw us staring. He gave a sick little laugh.

"What? What is it??"

What it was, was gross! Marco had green junk stuck between each of his teeth! It was spinach. Every time he opened his mouth to talk—which was all the time—green strings hung down!

My stomach rolled. Explosions, sleeping dogs, ghosts. Now this! I couldn't take any more. I jumped up from the table and ran straight to Tent Seven. Rolled tight in a sleeping bag, I closed my eyes and tried not to think.

Not about ghostly figures coming from

nowhere, not about poor Nosey zonked out on the path, not about sunstroke, and especially not about Marco with green in his teeth.

What I needed was sleep. Just sleep, sleep, sleep. A good night's sleep and I'd feel better in the morning. All of this would seem like just a very bad dream. That's it, just a nightmare.

The trouble was, I couldn't sleep.

Soon after dark, a flashlight beamed through the tent flap. I heard a familiar voice whining outside.

"Hey, Josh, let us in. It's me and Lolli and the twins. I got the brownies. We need to make plans. About the—well, you know!"

I had to give Marco credit. The little guy didn't give up easily. Besides, I was getting hungry. All I had was Mom's seaweed cookies, and I sure wasn't going to eat those!

I let them in.

Marco broke out the brownies. The rest of us ate, and he—what else?—talked.

"So here's my idea about what happened today," Marco said. "I think Skull brought that ghost to life. You know those chemicals he mixes? I think he's invented a ghost-summoning potion or something. Maybe he's a wizard, or a voodoo doctor! Maybe he's just pretending to be a camp director. Maybe he's really like Dr. Jekyll and Mr. Hyde. Hey, that's it! He's a mad scientist, and he's going to use the ghost to—"

Marco, the babbling brook, suddenly ran dry.

The brownie in my mouth had turned to cardboard. I couldn't swallow.

At that moment, you could have heard a mouse sneeze in Tent Seven.

Could it be? Was it possible? Dr. Skelnic sure looked scary enough. What was going on inside that skull of his? A million possibilities filled my head and spun around and around. I saw gray-smoke ghosts moving in on Camp Sea Dune. I saw blood-red eyes overpowering any living thing that got in the way. I saw—nothing but big trouble ahead. Really big trouble.

At last Marco broke the silence. His voice quivered.

"Josh . . . what are we going to do?"

There was only one thing we could do. Find out what evil scheme Skull had planned for

Camp Sea Dune. We decided to sneak over to the science lab first thing in the morning.

So we loaded our backpacks for action. Flashlights. Pocket knives. String. Compass. Whistles. It was really a pretty silly thing to do. None of that stuff would help if Dr. Skelnic had actually called up a real live ghost. But at least it gave us something to do while we waited for morning.

A sharp object bulged on the side of my pack. Oh yeah, Mom's seaweed cookies. I opened the tin box and began tossing the green balls into the bushes way behind the tent. Maybe the birds would eat these things.

Marco stopped me. "Hey, don't throw those cookies out! I want one! Seaweed is very nutritious, you know!"

He plopped a green ball into his mouth.

He chewed and chewed and chewed. He finally swallowed. "Not bad! You should try one, Josh. You never know, you just might like 'em!"

I shrugged and stuck the box of cookies back into my pack. I went over to tie the tent flaps shut. In the moonlight, Camp Sea Dune was beautiful. Everything seemed so peaceful and quiet. Nothing moved. Off in the distance, little ocean waves broke softly. Maybe we had imagined this whole ghost thing. Maybe it really was sunstroke. Maybe we had just stayed out on the beach too long.

But then I gasped. A man-shaped cloud of gray smoke suddenly appeared, in the very center of camp! It was the ghost. He was back!

"Guys!" I whispered. I motioned the others over to the door of the tent. "Look!"

Nervously, they all stuck their heads through the tent opening. I could hear four quiet gasps as they spotted the same smoky-gray man we had seen that afternoon. He was back!

The first time, the ghost had just hovered and then vanished. Now he roamed around, as if he were looking for something. His head was down, eyes to the ground. Great! I didn't want to have to look into those awful eyes again, ever!

"What's he's doing?" Lolli whispered.

The ghost crisscrossed the campfire area. He floated through solid log benches as if they weren't even there. He came to the camp bulletin board and passed right through to the other side. It was amazing. Nothing seemed to slow him down.

"Whatever he wants..." Gene murmured.

"...he wants real bad!" Dean finished.

"I read somewhere," Marco began, "that many ghosts have the power of transmogrification. They are able to—"

"Shut up!" I hissed. "He's coming this way!"

The ghost had left the campfire area. He was facing our way now, his eyes still to the ground. In the moonlight, I could see shadowy outlines of ragged clothing on his almost-transparent body. Was that shady thing under his chin a scraggly beard?

The ghost kept wandering around, looking from side to side. It was obvious he was searching for something. Or maybe someone.

Us? Was he coming for us?

The smoky figure came nearer and nearer. Each step brought him a little closer to our tent. Crouched beside me at the door, Dean and Gene gulped. Lolli's breath came faster and faster. I could feel sweat trickling down my back. But it was Marco who broke first.

"Qu-quick!" he stuttered. "Hide!"

He jumped up, knocking the rest of us off balance. Lolli landed on the floor with a heavy thud. We all scrambled in a tangle of arms and legs to get to our bunks. I pulled my sleeping bag over my head. I could hear someone whimpering. It had to be Marco.

Suffocating under the covers, I waited for something to happen. What would the ghost do to us? A picture of little Nosey, covered with gray sand, filled my head. What was that? Sand that made you sleep forever?

We waited and waited and waited.

Nothing.

We waited some more.

Silence.

I couldn't take the oven of my sleeping bag a moment longer. I threw back the covers and peered through the dark.

"Lolli? Dean, Gene? Marco? Are you guys all right?"

No answer. My heart skipped a beat. Had the ghost gotten them? What should I do?

Just then, a soft snore came from the direction of Lolli's bunk. I strained to listen. More regular breathing, the sound of peaceful sleep. That was Lolli. It just had to be. I'd know his breathing anywhere!

But then, a terrible thought crossed my mind. Was Lolli just sleeping a normal sleep? Or had the ghost coma-tized him with that gray sandy stuff? There was only one way to find out. As much as I dreaded it, I would have to get out of my sleeping bag and go over to Lolli's bunk.

And if the ghost was waiting there for me...

4

I reached into my backpack and fumbled around, feeling for my flashlight. A seaweed cookie rolled out. I knocked it out of the way and grabbed the light. I beamed it into every corner of the tent. Nothing. No gray wisps of smoke, anywhere. So far, so good.

I pulled one leg out of the sleeping bag and stepped onto the floor. I waited. Nothing happened. I swung my other leg down and stood up. Still nothing.

I inched across the tent, moving as quietly as I could. The space between my bunk and Lolli's seemed to grow as long as a football field. At last I reached Lolli's corner. I shone my flashlight right into his face.

Yes! He was OK! The bright beam of light told me what I wanted to know. He was fine. Oh, he was asleep all right, but I couldn't see one grain of that strange sand anywhere. Just plain old normal Lolli, snoring now like a freight train.

We were safe! The ghost had left us alone!

Just to make sure, I shook Lolli gently. "Hey, wake up, pal."

"Hmmm? J-Josh? 'Zat you? Go 'way," he mumbled. "Sleepy. Sle-e-e..."

He rolled over, out like a light.

I checked Dean and Gene and then went over to Marco's bunk. They were all sleeping like babies. Normal, healthy, un-sanded babies, that is!

I settled back down in my bunk to wait for morning. Tomorrow, one thing was for sure. We were definitely going to find out what sneaky business Skull was up to. Tent Seven would get to the bottom of this!

5

"No, no!" I moaned. I struggled to get free from the ropes that held me tight. I was sitting on a wooden bench by the campfire. My hands were tied behind my back. Lolli, also tied, sat on one side, Dean and Gene on the other.

A scream suddenly pierced the darkness. It

was coming from Marco.

Two large figures wearing hoods marched him up to the fire and pushed him down on the bench with us. "Watch this!" one of the figures snarled.

He turned to the fire and raised his arms, like a conductor directing an orchestra. He gestured violently. Flames shot high into the sky, sending up thick clouds of gray smoke. The figure waved his arms again, and the hood that covered his face slipped back.

I gasped. It was Skull! He looked at me and smiled. His teeth shone like tiny daggers in the firelight. Then he turned back toward the fire and pointed up at the thick clouds of smoke. As I watched, tiny red sparks of fire grew until they were the size of eyes. There were dozens of pairs of glowing eyes, staring right at me.

With his hands, Skull pulled the eyes out of the smoke. They became whole bodies, gray-smoke men created and controlled by the evil Dr. Skelnic!

The second hooded figure tipped his head back to howl at the moon. An evil cackle filled the night sky. I'd know that laugh anywhere. The second man was Max!

The gray-smoke men formed a line, with Skull at the front, and Max bringing up the rear. Their shadow feet stamped out a spooky rhythm on the sand. They turned away from the fire and marched toward the tents. I realized they were going after the rest of the campers.

"No! No!" I screamed. "Stop!"

I woke, drenched with sweat.

It was just a dream, a nightmare. It was absolutely crazy to think that Max and Dr. Skelnic were behind all this ghost stuff. Ridiculous. It couldn't be.

I wiped my face and tried to relax. But it was a long time before I fell back asleep.

In the morning, I woke to feel hot breath on my cheek.

It was Marco, whispering in my ear.

"Josh, is the ghost still out there? Is it safe to go outside? I gotta go to the bathroom—bad!"

He was sure hard to take, first thing in the morning. I groaned and rolled out of my bunk. Marco hung back while I peeked through the tent flap. I looked all around.

"Everything looks fine. No sign of the ghost anywhere. You can go now."

Marco just stared at me, pleading with those big brown eyes of his.

I finally got the message. "Oh, OK. Come on! I'll go with you."

The two of us crossed camp to the big bath-house. There was no sign that the ghost had been anywhere near the place.

By the time we got back to the tent, Marco was his old talkative self again. He burst through the tent flaps.

"Come on, twins, Lolli! Rise and shine! We've got a mystery to solve! There's nothing out there to be afraid of. We'll just talk to Dr. Skelnic and find out what's going on. It's probably just all one big misunderstanding, anyway. Get your back-packs on, and let's go!"

But Marco changed his tune pretty soon when we got to the lab.

Just to play it safe, we hid in a big clump of sea grass under the lab window. We had decided it would be smart to check things out before we went inside. From our hiding place, we could see

Dr. Skelnic hard at work, stirring something in a big glass jar.

The dark liquid foamed. Thousands of tiny bubbles rose to the top and fizzed. A smell like a million gym socks drifted out the open window. It was all we could do to keep from gagging.

I held my finger to my lips for silence. As we listened, Skull began muttering to himself.

"Now . . . if only I have the right formula . . . it was an accident the first time . . . got away from me before I knew . . . if this works . . . nothing will ever . . . ever . . . bother me again!"

We stared at each other. So it was Skull! He had made a potion that brought the ghost to life. And he was trying to do it again! We had to stop him!

I motioned to the open window overhead. Let's jump him, I mouthed. Lolli and the twins nodded in agreement. I was just about to give the signal when Marco sneezed.

It was one heck of a sneeze.

Inside the lab, we heard something glass hit the floor and shatter.

"Run!" I screamed.

But it was too late. A big hand reached out the

window and grabbed Marco by the hair.

"Just what I need!" Skull roared. "Guinea pigs. You boys get in here immediately!"

Dr. Skelnic didn't let go of Marco's hair until the rest of us had climbed the steps to the lab.

"Excellent, excellent! Marco, you may come in now." He smirked and rubbed his palms together. His hairless head gleamed in the bright lab light.

"Boys, your timing is perfect. I need to test my latest formula, and you five will do just fine. Stick out your arms!"

Lolli looked at me and gulped. The twins shifted closer together. Was this the ghost formula? Was the crazy doctor going to turn us all into ghosts? I whipped around to grab the flashlight from my backpack. If I swung it hard enough, maybe I could knock him out.

But it was too late.

Dr. Skelnic grabbed my arm. We struggled, and my backpack crashed to the floor. Dr. Skelnic wiped something cool-feeling on my arm.

I stared at the wet spot.

And waited to feel something—anything— that would tell me what was going to happen next.

7

Nothing happened.

Dr. Skelnic wiped some of his formula on each boy's arm.

But nothing happened. No change, no tingling, no sand, no ghosts.

Marco sniffed the green smudge on his arm. He stuck out his tongue and took a tiny lick of the formula. He smacked his lips. "Well, if it's a ghost-summoning formula, at least it tastes good!"

"A ghost-summoning formula? Is that what you think this is?" Dr. Skelnic collapsed into a chair, doubled over with laughter. A ghost formula! That's a good one!"

We looked at one another in puzzlement.

"So, just what is this stuff?" I asked, pointing to my arm.

Dr. Skelnic bent down and stuck the top of his skull head right in my face.

"Look closely. Do you see anything?" he suddenly demanded.

I examined his shiny bald scalp. "What am I supposed to be looking for?"

"Hair!" exclaimed the doctor, straightening up. "I think I have discovered a formula to grow hair! In the middle of my seaweed experiments, I stumbled onto something that I think will really work. If it does, millions and millions of people will buy my hair formula. I'll be rich, rich, rich! And famous!"

He suddenly grabbed the twins and started dancing around the room like a wild man.

Just as suddenly, he stopped.

"But what's this about a ghost formula? And why were you boys spying on me?"

We all started talking at once.

"Yesterday, an explosion—"

"Nosey fell asleep—"

"Air full of sand—"

"A gray-smoke man—"

"Last night, in the middle of the camp—"

Dr. Skelnic held up his hand. "Please, please! Let me see if I've got this straight. You think a ghost is here at Camp Sea Dune? A ghost who put Nosey to sleep with some strange kind of sand?"

He chuckled out loud. "I think you boys have been listening to too many of Max's crazy campfire stories!"

We stared at each other.

Max!

If Dr. Skelnic didn't have anything to do with the ghost, did that mean it was Max? We started to rush for the door.

"Wait! I'm coming with you!" Dr. Skelnic pulled off his lab coat.

We hadn't gone far down the path when we heard something crash in the lab. We all spun around to look. Then we heard another crash.

Dr. Skelnic moaned. "My work! My formula! I've got to go back!"

Marco stopped him. "Look!"

He pointed to the lab window. Through it, we could plainly see a gray shadow shaped like a man, crossing back and forth inside the room. It was the ghost! He was still looking for something. His smoky figure paced back and forth. Then it stopped and stared out the window in our direction.

The doctor gasped. "Is that what I think it is?"

I nodded. "Now do you believe us? There really is a ghost here at Camp Sea Dune!"

Skull turned and dashed through the bushes faster than I thought any grown-up could run.

"Come on!" he called over his shoulder. "We'd

better hope we can find Max. He's got to stop
that creature, before that creature stops us!"

We were too late.

The ghost had already found the camp.

All the kids had been sanded. Coma-tized.
Sent to some ghostly nightmare world for a long,
long nap.

It was the strangest sight I had ever seen.
Boys were all over the place, in the middle of all
the normal things they always did on a normal
morning at camp. Except—they were fast
asleep!

Everything was covered with that powdery
gray sand, the same stuff we had seen on Nosey.
The ghost had been here, all right.

Some boys had fallen asleep over breakfast in
the dining hall. They had their heads right down
in the pancakes on their plates. Maple syrup
dripped and ran, making trails in the gray sand
that blanketed everything.

Other guys dozed on top of the surfboards they
had been carrying down to the beach. Volleyball

players snored away on either side of the net. Some kids had fallen asleep beside the boat they were building, the hammers still in their hands.

The birds sang, the sun went right on shining, the beach towels hanging on the clothesline flapped in the breeze, but the campers were sleeping through it all.

If I hadn't been so scared, I would have laughed. Camp Sea Dune looked just like a ghost town from one of those old wild west movies.

Dr. Skelnic wasn't laughing either. He wandered around in a state of shock.

"My campers, my campers," he moaned. "I just don't understand. How did the ghost do this? How could all of them be asleep?"

He knelt down and grabbed a handful of the mysterious gray sand that covered everything. He sifted it thoughtfully between his fingers. You could almost hear the wheels start turning in that mad scientist brain of his.

"Odd," he said, "this sand is quite unlike any other sand I have ever seen. Boys! Check all the tents. See if there is anyone still awake! Look for clues that might tell us what happened here. Hurry! We don't have any time to waste. If this sand is what I think it is . . ."

The sober look on his face told us the rest of the story. We started off to check tents. The doctor called after us.

"And keep an eye out for the ghost! I don't think he will come back to a place he's already searched, but we don't know that for certain. Maybe Max can tell us—if we ever find him!"

The twins, Lolli, Marco and I rushed from tent to tent, turning back flaps covered with the powdery gray stuff. No luck. Not one kid in camp had managed to stay awake.

We did find something, though. Over in Tent Three, Marco spotted something green clenched in the fist of a sleeping boy.

"Josh, look over here. I've seen this green stuff somewhere before. What is it?"

I couldn't believe my eyes. Part of a small green ball showed between the boy's curled fingers. It was one of my mom's seaweed cookies! How on earth did this kid get my cookie? Then I remembered. I had thrown some of them out in the bushes the night before. This kid must have spotted the cookie and picked it up. Poor guy. I'll bet he was real disappointed when he tasted it!

"Josh, Dr. Skelnic should see this," Marco said. "It might be a clue."

I snorted. "It's only a stale health food cookie, Marco. Trust me, it can't possibly be a clue. We're looking for ghost stuff, remember?"

But Marco insisted. So we pried open the boy's hand and removed the small green ball. We were just handing it over to Skull when we heard a sudden crashing sound on the other side of the camp. It was like an bronco bull was heading right our way.

"No! No! Please, no!" a voice screamed.

It sounded like Max.

We took off in the direction of the scream.

"No! Please, no!" the voice begged again.

Just what were we going to see on the other side of camp? Had the ghost found Max?

Dean and Gene got there first. The rest of us crowded around, half afraid to look.

Max was sitting on the ground at the very edge of the tent area. His head was slumped on his chest. His eyes were closed. His hands hung down by his sides. We were too late. The ghost had sanded Max.

Or at least that's what we thought.

Then Lolli noticed something.

"Hey, wait a minute! Where's all the sand, that stuff the ghost uses to make people fall asleep?" Lolli knelt down to look closer. "If there's no sand, then Max must be all right!"

Lolli grabbed Dr. Skelnic's assistant by the shoulder.

"Max? Max, it's me, Lolli. Talk to us, Max. What happened?"

At last, Max lifted his head. There was a horrible expression of fear on his face. That's when he saw us for the first time. He was speechless for several seconds. But finally, a sound came out of his mouth.

"Gh-ghost! Ghost!" he croaked.

Dr. Skelnic took over. "What do you know about the ghost, Max?" he demanded. "Tell me!"

The young man tried to speak, but no other sound would come out of his mouth. He swallowed and tried again.

"Gray shadows. Red eyes. Horrible red eyes." Max closed his eyes and shuddered. He took a deep breath and looked like he was going to fall asleep.

Dr. Skelnic shook him hard. "Max, please! It's

a matter of life and death! You've got to tell us what happened. Try again!"

Max straightened up. "I—I had gone to the lab to look for you, Doctor. But when I got there, the place was covered with awful gray sand. Piles of it, all over the place. So I started to come here. I had just reached the edge of the clearing when something dark and smoky came rushing up. It was a ghost, a man with fiery eyes that cut through my brain. The pain—oh, the pain! I just knew I was going to die. I fell down here. That's all I remember. Then you came."

Dr. Skelnic stared at his assistant for a long hard moment. "So," he said at last, "you didn't do anything to summon the ghost to Sea Dune?"

Max was stunned. "Me?" He looked really bewildered. "I don't know anything about calling up ghosts! Whatever gave you that idea?"

Dean and Gene glared at him.

"Your campfire stories," Dean said.

Gene continued. "All those stories about—"

"The monster who ate campers?"

"The vampire that sleeps in the lab?"

"The slasher who hid out in the dunes?"

"The alien who wanted to take boys to her planet?"

The twins were giving it to Max with both barrels. He still looked horrified.

"Guys, Dr. Skelnic! You gotta believe me! Those were just silly stories that I made up. You know, make-believe, pretend? I don't know a thing about any real ghosts. Honest!"

A sudden searing heat flashed down my spine. Boy, that sure felt creepy! I shook it off and tried to tune back in to the discussion between Max and the others.

"You mean, the whole camp's got sand piled everywhere? What are we going to do? We can't even use the radio to call for help. It was trashed when the ghost hit the lab."

There! I felt it again. Something like a red-hot knife drew a line down my backbone. I looked over my shoulder. Nothing there. Just my overactive imagination.

The guys kept talking, but the pounding in my ears drowned out their words. Something weird was happening here, something I definitely did not like!

I turned around and peeked into the bushes. Then I saw them—those sizzling red eyes. It was the ghost! He was back, and he wanted me! I'm not sure how I knew that, but his eyes seemed to draw me to him. I wanted to step away from the group and go closer. I felt an unexplainable urge to go to him, I moved further and further away. . . .

"Hey, Josh!" Marco's piercing voice cut through my brain. "Where are you going? Oh, no! The ghost! He's back! Come on, Josh, run! Now!"

10

We ended up in the camp storage shed.

I don't remember running.

I only know my arms ached where the others had dragged me away from those terrible hypnotizing eyes. My back hurt where my pack had bounced up and down. And my sneakers were full of sand spurs, those tiny stickers that grow on the beach.

"Wow! Thanks, you guys! That was close!"

They nodded, dropped their backpacks, and sprawled on the floor. Max and Dr. Skelnic found old buckets and flipped them over to use for stools. Everyone looked exhausted. This horror business was about to wear us out. But if the ghost had his way, we'd all take a nice l-o-n-g nap. Maybe permanently.

I rolled over on my back and stretched my arms. They sure were sore. A funny-looking spot on my arm caught my eye. Was that a bruise? I looked closer. No. It was where Dr. Skelnic had swabbed me with his hair-growth formula.

The potion had dried to form a thin crust one shade greener than my skin. I rubbed the spot with my finger. It felt really soft, like. . . . Was it possible? Was that fuzz hair? Could the doctor's formula really make hair grow?

"Guys, check this out!" I cried. "Are you growing hair? I think I am!"

Dr. Skelnic rushed to my side. The other boys examined their own arms. We all showed the same results—soft spots covered with tiny new greenish hairs. Skull had done it! He really was going to be rich and famous!

At least one good thing was happening during this nightmare we were trapped in. We started thinking of all the ways Skull could spend the fortune he was surely going to make on his hair-growth formula.

"I know, buy a yacht and sail around the world!" Lolli said.

"No, Dr. Skelnic wouldn't waste his money on that," argued Marco. "He'll build a state-of-the-art science lab here on the island."

"Get a fancy sports car," said Gene.

"And a mansion," suggested Dean.

"Maybe he'll buy a TV station and start his own science show," I said. I admit, we were getting a little carried away. But it sure felt good to think about something instead of the terrifying ghost for a while.

Besides, Max burst our bubble soon enough.

He and Dr. Skelnic had moved near the door of the shed, where the light was the best. Skull had his bald head down, and Max was checking it with the magnifying glass he always carried in his pocket.

"Well?" Skull demanded. "Tell me. Do you see any hair? I first used the formula two days ago, so the hairs should be longer than the fuzz on the boys' arms. Do you see anything?"

Max drew a deep breath. "Yes. I do. But I'm afraid it's not hair. Wait just a minute and I'll show you." He gave a quick jerk on something near the Doctor's scalp.

"Ow-w-w-w! Max, did you just pull out one of my new hairs?" The doctor rubbed his head. He looked pretty angry to me.

Max grinned that goofy smile of his. "I pulled something out all right, but it wasn't hair. Look—you were growing seaweed!" He held up a thin green strand of something that looked a lot like hair, except that it was fuzzier.

"Congratuations, Doctor! You've finally done it. You've discovered the formula for growing seaweed!"

Skull's face was a funny mixture of excitement and disappointment. I felt the same way. When you thought you had a million-dollar hair-growth product on your hands, a formula for sea-weed seemed pretty worthless.

Seaweed? Was that what was forming on my arm? Seaweed? I used some grains of beach sand to scrub the pale green fuzz off my arm. Dr. Skelnic bent over again and told Max to pull out the rest of the seaweed growing on his scalp. From the moans he made, those strands must have had very deep roots!

Max calmly flicked the few seaweed "hairs" out the door of the shed. None of us realized then the power of those tiny green threads.

11

Listening to the doctor's moans and groans made me shiver. I thought about all the kids sleeping back at camp, covered with that mysterious gray sand. What did they feel like? Did they wonder—in their dreams—what had happened to them? Would they ever wake up?

The crinkle of a candy wrapper broke the silence in the shed. At least good old Lolli was still awake!

He grinned. "Guess what? I have a new name for the camp. Not Sea Dune, but Sea Doom. Get it—doom—as in danger? Come spend a summer at Camp Sea Doom, for the thrills and chills of a lifetime! Ha-ha-h...."

He stopped in mid-laugh and froze.

All eyes stared at the entrance to the shed.

What had Lolli seen? Was it our turn now? Was the ghost finally coming for us? I didn't know how much more of the tension any of us could take. My nerves were like rubber bands, stretched to the absolute breaking point.

Marco was the first to snap.

"Oh, no, no!" he shrieked. "I can't stand another minute of this. Somebody get me out of here! Please! Come on, let's go, before the ghost gets here. I'm not kidding. Where can we go? The camp's been hit, the lab, everywhere. I just know we're gonna die!"

He turned to me. "Josh, I don't want to die. You're the brave one. Please, please, get me out of here. I'm begging you. Right now, before—

"What's that?" he screamed. And then he passed out.

I spun around. My eyes were everywhere at once. I searched for evil red eyes and wisps of gray smoke. I stuck out my hand to test the air for bits of stinging gray sand.

Nothing. No smoke, no evil eyes, no sand, no ghost. Nothing.

But there was Marco, limp as a wet noodle, out cold on the floor.

We helped him sit up. His head had hit the floor pretty hard when he fell. Now he had a knob on it the size of a walnut. Ouch. I almost felt sorry for him. We were all scared. But losing control wasn't going to help anything.

I had a bad feeling that things at Camp Sea Dune were going to get worse—a lot worse—before they started to get better.

12

"So, what do you call a kid's lousy vacation? I'll give you one clue. It rhymes with 'summer camp.' Give up? It's easy—bummer camp!"

Lolli tried another joke to cheer us up. He bombed again. Nobody laughed.

We sat and stared out the shed door. Marco held his throbbing head.

Max tried next. He started one of his corny campfire stories.

"Once upon a time," he said, "and far away on a mysterious island in a storybook sea, there lived a—"

"Wait, Max! That's it!!"

Dr. Skelnic jumped to his feet. He began pacing back and forth inside the shed.

"Once upon a time...that's it! That's the key we need to figure out what's going on around here. Once upon a time. Why didn't I think of that? Max, you're brilliant!"

The goofy assistant looked puzzled, but pleased. "I am?"

Skull scrubbed the sore spots on his bald head in excitement. "Think, Max! Use your cerebellum oblongata! Think of every old story you've ever heard about this island! What do the old-timers say about this place? What went on here, years ago? Did something bad happen? What was this island like, once upon a time?"

Max still looked confused.

"I get it!" Marco was on his feet now, too. "The ghost is probably connected to something that happened here in the past. When we figure that out, we'll know how to send him back to where he belongs."

Marco walked over and shook Max by the shoulder. "It's simple, Max. All you have to do is start telling stories. The true ones."

A light bulb went off in Max's brain.

"Right, right! Now I get it! OK, let's see. Bad things that really happened here on the island. True stories. H-m-m-m. Well, there have been lots of hurricanes, shipwrecks on the beach, buried treasure . . ."

He paused, lost in thought. "I've got it," he said at last, speaking slowly. "The hermit. The strange old hermit who lived all alone here on the island. Why didn't I think of him before now? Let me see. How did that story go . . . ?"

13

While Max worked on remembering, Marco opened his backpack. He brought out the rest of his goodies from home.

That rich chocolatey smell hit me in the pit of my stomach. Brownies! Marco's mom had sent heaven in a box! We were all starved. Everyone dived in, even Dr. Skelnic and Max.

Those brownies were exactly what we needed to get our spirits up again.

At last, Max remembered the story.

We munched and listened.

"The old people around here," Max began, "tell of a ship that wrecked on the rocks that circle this island. Unfortunately, only one man made it to shore. All the other sailors drowned in the rough waves, which smashed the ship into matchsticks. The man was left with nothing but the clothes on his back, and he nearly died.

"But little by little, day by day, he slowly got used to living here. He learned to live off the bounty of the sea. There were always plenty of fish and crabs and turtles to catch. The man even learned to like seaweed. Back in those days, lots of seaweed, several different varieties of it, used to wash up on shore. The man would mix it with raw seagull eggs for breakfast, or bake it in the sun to use as bread."

Lolli groaned. "That's disgusting! Eating seaweed? Yuck! I've never been that hungry!"

I didn't remember the cookies in my backpack until that very moment! I opened the tin box and passed it to Dr. Skelnic. He tried one.

"Say, these are pretty good!" He tossed a green ball to Max. "Here!"

Something must happen to your taste buds when you grow up. Adults eat such weird things—tofu, coffee, asparagus, liver, seaweed!

Max continued with his story.

"So anyway, the years went by. Many ships passed near the island, but none of them stopped. No one knew the man was marooned here. At last, a ship with a leak stopped so the sailors could make repairs. They found the man, now very old and set in his peculiar island ways.

"The sailors promised they would take the man home. But when the repairs to their ship were finished, the old man had disappeared. They searched the whole island, but he was nowhere to be found."

Dean and Gene had a question.

"What happened—"

"Did he die?"

Max shrugged. "No one knows. He just up and disappeared."

I turned to Dr. Skelnic. "Do you think the ghost we've been seeing is actually the hermit from Max's story? If that's true, why has he decided to come back and bother us? Why doesn't he stay by himself, like he did when he was alive?"

Skull reached for another seaweed cookie.

"It's possible that—"

Marco interrupted, a wild look on his face. "I've got it! Listen to this. This is it. It has to be!"

He paused to make sure we all were listening. "If you were the hermit, and you had been dead for a long, long time, what would you want most when you came back to life?" We stared blankly.

"Think, Lolli!" Marco said. "What would you want?"

Lolli laughed. "That's easy. Candy! You really think the ghost wants candy?"

"Not just candy. Food!" Marco cried. "He wants any kind of food!"

"You know," Dr. Skelnic said thoughtfully,

"Marco just might be right. The ghost could be looking for food. Since we keep all the food in the refrigerator, there's no way he can get at it. I've read that ghosts can pass through organic matter, like wood and stone, but they can't handle mixed materials like steel or tin."

Marco grinned. "So it's simple! All we have to do is open the fridge. Then the ghost can eat all he wants. He'll get full, and he'll go away."

No one spoke for a minute. We were all testing Marco's plan in our heads. Could it be possible? Was the solution to our enormous problem as simple as that? One person would walk back to the kitchen, open up the refrigerator, and get out of the way. Easy.

There was just one drawback.

The ghost.

What if he attacked before the person ever got to the kitchen? It would be like walking straight into the mouth of a hungry lion, almost a suicide mission.

But it was our only hope, our only idea for ridding Camp Sea Dune of this terrible creature from the island's past.

Who would be brave enough to do it?

Who would be the one to open the refrigerator? Who would trap the ghost?

14

"We'll go." Dean and Gene said it first, together. The twins were tough.

"No! I'm the director of this camp. I should go," said Skull.

"But your scientific work is too important," argued Max. "I should go."

"Forget it, everybody. I'm going, and that settles it," I said.

Lolli protested. "I'm bigger and stronger than you are, Josh. I'll go."

There was a moment's pause. Then Marco said in a high, squeaky voice, "Well, I suppose I could go. It was my idea. So, I—I guess I should be the one to do it. That is, if you guys really want me to."

A giggle escaped from me. I knew it wasn't nice, but I couldn't help it. Even when Marco tried to be brave, he sounded like a scared little mouse. I laughed out loud.

He glared at me.

"We're all scared, Marco! We're just timid little mice!" I laughed again, but it wasn't a happy laugh.

The next second, all of us were laughing our heads off, even Skull and Max. We were all scared. It was the truth. Nobody wanted to go up to the kitchen alone.

"Let's just go together," I said, when the nervous laughter stopped. "The more of us watching out for the ghost, the better."

Everyone nodded.

"And we'd better take our backpacks, just in case. You never know what we might need."

I bent down and picked up my tin of seaweed cookies. Max's hand shot out just as I started to push the lid down. He grabbed a green ball and stuffed it into his shirt pocket.

"I'll take one more of those," he grinned, "for the road!"

Our packs on our backs, we stopped at the shed door to shake hands all around. All our faces were pale and serious. It looked like we were at a funeral, except that no one had died. At least not yet.

Quickly, we headed back to camp. Seven pairs of legs pounded the trail. Seven pairs of eyes searched the bushes as we moved. Seven hearts pounded hard in seven throats. Seven mouths tasted like cotton. Where was the ghost? Would we all make it to the kitchen?

Every second of the way, I thought I would feel those eyes of fire burn into my body. At each turn in the path, I watched for that hot stinging sand that could bring endless nightmares.

But before I knew it, we were there. I looked in amazement at the others. We were all there! Dr. Skelnic, Max, Lolli, Marco, the twins. We had all made it safely to the kitchen! And no sign of the ghost, anywhere! The impossible dream was about to become reality. Once we got inside the kitchen, that ghost would be ancient history again!

"Go ahead, Max," Skull urged. "You've got the keys. Unlock the door, quick!" Max groaned, a sick look on his face. "Aren't the keys in your pocket? I don't have them."

Dr. Skelnic frantically checked every pocket. Nothing. He hurriedly pointed to a small window just below the kitchen roof.

"You boys will have to get in that way. Max and I will help you up. There's a combination lock on the refrigerator door. 47 Right, 52 Left,

33 Right, 16 Left. And be careful, that fridge door is extremely heavy."

He was talking so fast, the numbers tangled in my brain.

"Marco, you remember the combination. Lolli, you handle the door. Twins, you stand guard inside. Josh, you keep everybody together. Go!"

Skull bent down and made a step with his hands. A mighty heave from below and I was through the kitchen window.

Once inside, we went straight to our positions, like soldiers trained for battle. Marco and Lolli worked on the lock. Dean and Gene patrolled the large room. I stood on top of a table I pushed under the window. That way I could see all the action, both inside the kitchen and outside where Skull and Max stood guard.

I took a moment to catch my breath. Things were going just great, even without keys. A few more moments and we'd have the refrigerator door open!

But that was the moment our luck ran out.

A sudden movement outside caught my eye. Before I even had time to blink, the ghost materialized out of thin air, at the very spot where Max and the doctor were standing.

"Watch out!" I started to scream.

But it was already over. In a split second, the ghost had raised one smoky arm and pointed at the two men. The fiery eyes blazed. Millions of particles of sand suddenly shot from his fingertips!

Skull and Max put up their arms to protect their faces, but it didn't help. Gray sand started piling up all around their feet. They yawned. They groaned. They sagged, fast asleep.

The ghost had gotten them!

15

"Quick!" I screamed. "Get that fridge door open!"

Marco's fingers flew, twisting the dial on the lock, first to the right and then to the left. I heard a loud metal click as he yanked the lock open. Lolli grabbed the handle of the enormous door, heaving like Hercules. The fridge swung open with a heavy groan.

"Grab something and throw it here," I ordered. "The ghost is right outside. He just got Skull and Max!"

Lolli slung a big chunk of raw meat in my direction. I caught it and clawed at the clear plastic wrap. Yuck. I couldn't get a firm hold. Then finally gripping the wet beef firmly in my hand, I poked my arm out the kitchen window.

If that ghost was hungry, a big steak dinner should keep him busy for a while, I thought.

I aimed right for the ghost and heaved. The steak wobbled a short distance through the air, then fell with a sickening thud. It was a miserable throw. I didn't get the steak close enough to him to attract the ghost's attention.

But then again, maybe I had. He turned to look in my direction. The glowing coals of his eyes looked down at the meat, and then up at me. I suddenly couldn't think any more. I had no will power of my own left. Those eyes held me prisoner with their intense fire. The ghost didn't want that steak.

He didn't want anything but me.

And I couldn't move.

16

Inside the kitchen, Lolli, the twins, and Marco rushed over to the table where I stood. I felt their hands on my legs.

"We gotta get Josh down from there, away from those eyes." It was Marco. He was the only one to realize what was happening to me.

The guys pulled me off the table. Dean and Gene led us across the kitchen to a door on the other side. There was a path that led down to the beach, away from camp. Away from the ghost.

I ran my guts out. All of us did. Each breath cut through my lungs like a knife. My backpack slammed into me with every step.

We hadn't gone more than a few yards when we saw the ghost.

He followed us, all the way to the beach. He could have gotten us at any time, but he didn't. He always stayed behind, watching, waiting for something. What was it? *What*?

We came to the end of the trail. Here, the ground stopped, forming a steep bank that dropped ten feet to the beach below. Without a moment's hesitation, the five of us jumped. We landed in a jumble of arms, legs, and elbows on the sand at the bottom.

I expected the ghost to float down any second, to cover us with the same terrible sand that held the rest of the camp hostage.

We waited. And waited. And waited. The ghost never came.

Lolli jerked his head toward the bank and whispered, "I'm crawling up to check things out. This waiting is driving me crazy!"

The big kid inched up the sand bank and peeped over the ledge. In a few minutes he was back down.

"He's still there. He's waiting for something, I guess, 'cause he just moves back and forth like he's pacing. But he's got us trapped good. With him up there and the ocean right there, we can't move!"

The hours ticked by. The other boys took turns checking on the ghost. He stayed up on the ledge, moving back and forth. Watching. Waiting. Never coming any closer. If something didn't happen soon, we'd all be crazy.

Something did happen. We fell asleep.

17

The sun was hot. I opened my eyes. For a minute, I couldn't remember where I was. Then it all came back to me.

"Hey!" I laughed. "I'm awake! I'm actually awake!"

I looked down at my arms and legs. No mysterious gray sand on me anywhere. Just normal beach sand, from sleeping down by the ocean.

I woke up the others.

"Get up, guys! It's morning, and we're OK. We're still OK!"

Lolli, Marco, and the twins yawned. They stretched out the kinks. None of us had meant to go to sleep, not with a ghost waiting at the top of the bank.

"Josh, is he still there?" Marco asked.

I was feeling brave in the morning sunshine. "Let's go see."

The two of us scrambled up the bank. We peeked over the sandy dune with its clumps of grass and shrubs. It would be hard to see a ghost made of gray smoke in the hot bright light.

Something moved.

"There he is!" I pointed. "He's still there. If we only knew what he wanted. We can't stay here much longer. We'll go nuts."

The two of us watched the ghost march back and forth across the dune. He was little more than a thin outline of air, only slightly darker than everything else.

"Come on," I said. "We might as well tell the others."

"You go," Marco said. "I'm going to stay here and think for a minute. There's gotta be something we can do." Marco sure had changed over the last few days.

I slid down the bank with the bad news.

Lolli just stared. "Hungry," he mumbled. "I'm hungry."

"Me, too," said Dean.

"Me, too," echoed Gene.

"Sorry, guys. I don't think there is anything lef—" I suddenly remembered the health food cookies in my backpack. Was Lolli hungry enough to eat seaweed?

I grabbed the tin and opened the lid. "Josh!" Marco suddenly called down from the ledge. "Something's happening! He's coming! The ghost is coming closer!"

Marco rolled down the bank in a panic. He saw the open tin of seaweed cookies in my hand. A look of intense concentration filled his face. He slammed the lid back down on the cookie tin.

Then he exploded. "I know what he wants,

Josh! Seaweed! The ghost wants your mom's seaweed cookies!"

"Wh-what?" I didn't get it.

But there wasn't time to explain.

Marco was trying to push me up the bank. "We've got to give him those cookies!"

"Well, here! Take them." I held the tin out to Marco.

He shook his head. "You're the athlete, Josh. I can't throw hard enough. We need to get the cookies to the ghost before he comes any closer. If we give him all the cookies, he'll go away for good. At least I think he will. You do it, Josh. You're our only hope."

He looked back at the bank. "But you have to do it now. Right now!"

Lolli and the twins came and stood by Marco. They started to cheer, "Go, Josh! Go, Josh! Go, Josh!"

I still didn't get it, but there wasn't time to think. I just had to trust Marco on this one.

I climbed the sand bank, with the tin of cookies in my hand. Slowly, I peered over the edge. The ghost was waiting. I put one foot on top of the ledge and pulled myself up.

My heart banging in my chest, I stood to face him.

The intense red heat of his eyes hit me like a tidal wave!

"Josh, take off the lid and throw the can," Marco yelled from down below.

My hand trembled as I pulled off the lid.

Suddenly, the light streaming from the ghost's eyes intensified. All I could think of was sleep. I desperately wanted to sleep.

No, I told myself. I had to shake it off. I had to fight off this terrible wall of sleep the ghost was building around me. But I couldn't move!

Marco's voice broke through the cobwebs in my brain.

"Throw 'em, Josh. He wants seaweed!"

My sluggish brain stumbled. Seaweed...? What seaweed...? Oh yeah, Mom's health food cookies....

I could hear Lolli and the twins, "Go, Josh, go!"

The ghost came closer and closer. Slowly, he began to stretch his arm toward me. All I could think of was sleeping. I was so tired.

Marco screamed again. "Throw the cookies now!"

It was a struggle to move at all. But I did it.

With my last ounce of strength, I got my arm back in throwing position. I aimed straight for those red glowing eyes. With a big groan, I heaved the open cookie tin as hard as I could.

It was the pass of a lifetime. A pro quarterback couldn't have done better.

The tin box flew into the air like a guided missile. It arched up and hung in the sky for a second. Then it whizzed down, gaining speed like a bullet, straight into the outstretched arms of the ghost!

There was an ear-splitting clap of thunder, followed by a flash of lightning. Cool drops of rain began to fall.

The ghost was gone.

18

It rained all afternoon. The rain washed the island clean. Little by little, Camp Sea Dune came back to life.

We splashed around in the rain, whooping and screaming like wild men! The first to wake up was our camp mascot, Nosey. He met us on the path back to the tents, bouncing and yipping and licking.

Soon, sleeping kids everywhere were yawning and stretching. They went right back to the things they had been doing before the ghost passed by—playing volleyball, hammering nails, carrying surfboards down to the beach. Nobody even asked why the breakfast was cold!

Last to awaken were Dr. Skelnic and Max. It was all so strange. They couldn't remember anything either. Only the guys in Tent Seven knew how close Camp Sea Dune had come to being a ghost town forever.

That night after supper, the five of us went down to the beach to figure things out.

"Are you going to tell me why those cookies worked?" I asked Marco. "I still don't get it."

"When the ghost wouldn't eat that steak, I started thinking. He was the hermit in Max's story, right? Well, after spending all those years eating nothing but seaweed, that's what he was used to. He wouldn't come back as a ghost and want steak or sandwiches or brownies. What would he want? More seaweed. The trouble is, nowadays, no seaweed grows on this island. The only seaweed around here was in your mom's health food cookies."

I scratched my head. "OK, but why did the ghost sand everybody else, if all he wanted was my cookies?"

Dean and Gene knew the answer for this one. "Nosey got sanded—"

"Because he had a seaweed cookie in his mouth."

"And remember," Lolli added, "you scattered some of the cookies outside the tent for the birds. That's how the other campers got sanded."

I snapped my fingers. "That's why Skull and Max got it, too. Max had a seaweed cookie in his pocket!"

Marco nodded. "There at the end, when the ghost followed us, he was waiting for someone to open the tin box. He couldn't get the cookies on his own. When you made that amazing pass, he finally got enough of the food he craved. Face it, Josh, you're a hero! You sent the ghost home!"

"Aw, cut it out," I growled. "I never would have figured it out. You're the hero, Marco. And you know what we do to heroes around here!"

I grabbed his arms. Lolli and the twins got his legs. We threw him, kicking and screaming, but laughing, into the waves. The old Marco would have whined and cried. The new Marco loved every minute of it!

We had just flopped down on the sand when we heard it—an explosion that rocked the beach. High in the sky over Dr. Skelnic's lab rose a cloud of green smoke.

"Oh, no," Dean moaned.

"Here we go again!" Gene groaned.